Liberté

Daniel Parker

ISBN: 1492301167
ISBN-13: 978-1492301165

DEDICATION

For all the women in my life,
for their sufferings in a man's world,
and the blessings they give in return.

CONTENTS

ACKNOWLEDGMENTS

This story began as a screenplay written nearly a decade ago, yet this is the first time it has been brought to the public in any form. The War of 1812 is one of those points in history about which most Americans know very little and how close our young country came to a premature ending. Great writers of history did the hard work and left wonderful and awe-inspiring accounts of events, and I use these writings as background for the introduction of our French heroine. Last but certainly not least, I want to thank the readers and editors who have assisted me over the years, including Bruce Ballister, Adrian Fogelin, Douglas Hattaway, David Mitchell, Jack Pittman, Julianne Price, and Richard Rubino. Special thanks goes to Constance G. Burt for her wonderful editing on this particular book. Finally, to my beautiful family, who give me the time, space and inspiration to write.

1 RISE

The years closing the eighteenth century and beginning the next were as bloody and momentous as world history would record. Countries fought for elbow space and men killed to become gods. The world was a battlefield with the smell of death and ambition and lust encircling a new kind of freedom: a freedom of thought and actions that threatened the established order of both the church and the nobility. It was the success of the Americans that challenged the order of things. Revolution and patriotism escaped from the former colonies and swept across the ocean into all of old Europe, cleansing the land with the blood of martyrs and kings.

The great French general Napoleon Bonaparte was keen on taking advantage of this movement and he was ripe to do it. Liberty was all the excuse he needed. He did what no one else could do. He tried what no one else was willing to try. And little did he know how much fruit his seeds would eventually bear.

It started deep in the south of France where the families of liberty paid a heavy price for Napoleon's ambition. The monarchists were sent packing by the revolutionaries, and their European neighbors of royalty were scared of being next. Who was this usurping general? Who dared to question the order of things? Their consensus was to go on the offense before things got out of hand, and take the war to the man himself, before he ran rough over the whole of the world.

The French inhabitants of the small towns and villages had little say in these decisions. With their men conscripted to fight, the women and children carried on in the fields and the shops until the war came home. When it did, they ran and hid under a barrage of cannon and blades before they, too, became collateral damage.

Some were too late – always too late – and fell in the street. Some protected their land and their homes and their families in the name of liberty and forfeited their lives. If no one was looking, many were simply shot for greed or sport.

Some crimes could be even worse.

The girl was nine years old when a fate beyond her control sent her on a different journey. She ran when her mother told her to. She lost sight of her sisters and brothers and ran to the mill where the nooks and ledges could hide someone her size. She wasn't the first to think of the mill. When she entered, the smell overwhelmed her and she covered her face. The flies were going to work on the bodies, some whom she recognized, and she suppressed her fear and revulsion. She heard a noise outside and with no time to climb, she dropped to the floor, knee deep in death. She tucked in between a body still warm with blood and the cold cobblestone beneath. Two English soldiers entered the open doorway.

"Aah! It already stinks," one protested.

They stepped roughly, using their bayonets to stab for any remaining life as they pilfered the bodies for gold. Yet most of the dead were empty of wealth.

"Blech! These bastards are poor," said the other soldier. "Not worth me time."

He forced opened the mouth of a dead man with little hair and fat arms and struck gold. He used his fingers and a homemade tool to pry loose the shiny crown. He was proud of his mining when he noticed movement. He smiled and reached a hand into the pile of bodies and pulled the girl out.

She screamed and kicked. Her dark hair hid her dark eyes – eyes that had already seen too much. The English soldier moved the hair from her face and saw the freckly skin and almond-shaped eyes.

"Mademoiselle," he said.

She kicked and screamed for her freedom.

"You'll have to hurry, mate," said the other soldier. He looked out the open doorway while the other soldier pinned her and began to unbutton his pants.

2

"Hold still, you squirmy little bitch!" he demanded.

It was awkward, holding the girl down and trying to unbutton with one hand, so he hit her across the face and she fell limp. He was hungry with lust and ignored the smelly carcasses and the flying insects as he rushed to get his pants down. He was on top of her quickly and the girl, coming to her senses, pushed against him and squirmed. Then she felt something hard and cold and she screamed. He muffled her cries with one hand. Her own hands dug into the floor, searching the bodies around her. Her fingers found something hidden in clothing – a blade. She grabbed the blade and wrenched it free. While the attacker was trying to steal a few moments of ecstasy, she stabbed.

"AAAAAHHH," he yelled.

She stabbed again and again and again, and was quickly covered in the Englishman's blood.

The other soldier gaped in shock and fright as she pushed the weight of the man off of her. The soldier rose up with a face full of agony and he fell dead into the ass of another man. She stood up, drenched in blood and still armed with the dripping blade. The living soldier saw a little devil – something he did not want to provoke further. He bolted through the doorway and ran.

The girl looked around her. She was the only one breathing. *What madness has occurred here? Why is this happening to me?* A shot in the distance startled her attention and she walked outside with the knife still extended.

The other English soldier lay dead in the street. He hadn't made it far. A group of masked soldiers rode by on horseback with their guns at the ready. But this was not just any cavalry – it was Napoleon's personal guard – the secret and the unknown. They had dark uniforms, strong horses, the best weaponry. The girl had seen soldiers and killing instruments before, but nothing like this.

One soldier stood out from the rest by her long dark hair flowing from behind a mask of painted skull bones. The eyes behind the mask looked at the girl, who was frightened but couldn't turn away. The killer was a woman and streaks of blood covered the unusual armor and only the eyes betrayed that she was still human. Her sword was strapped to her back instead of her side. The girl stared until the woman warrior was gone with the rest to inflict more damage.

The girl stood alone again while the sounds of war continued in the distance. Before long, the click of boots and clatter of hooves announced the approach of yet another group of soldiers. This formation filled the street with the blue and white of the French regular army. Two soldiers kicked the bodies of their red-and-white clad enemies to confirm their deaths. As they rode and marched past the girl, she had enough sense to move to the side. They paid her little attention. She watched the procession of hundreds of troops until it ended and the street was soon empty of life again.

One more rider approached, this one alone and taking his time. His horse meandered as he observed the kills of the day. He stopped to look from the comfort of his saddle. He was dressed in his French blue and white colors, and his black hat stood tall on his head. He took a sip from a flask and then noticed the girl. He kicked his heel and the horse trotted toward her. He saw the bloody blade in her hand, imagining what the girl witnessed and the act she committed.

He halted his horse. Through the open door of the mill, he could see the carnage. He stared into the girl's eyes. She stared back at him, frozen by the imposing figure on the horse. He reached his hand down to her and motioned for her to take it. She looked at him, and a part of her trusted what she saw, so she placed her hand in his.

Young Josephine was nothing in the spoils and destruction of war. As fate would have it, the day she lost everything was the day she was reborn. Napoleon took the newly orphaned girl and sent her to be trained. He sent her to become like the woman warrior she had seen that fateful day. To become a killer in Napoleon's personal guard.

Napoleon handed her off to a soldier with a set of orders, who in turned handed her to another, and so it continued until she found herself stuffed into a burlap bag and transported far away from the home she knew. Reaching her final destination, she was tossed off the back of an old ox cart still stuffed inside the bag. She was jammed between the other deliverables – bags full of rice and dry goods and bolts of cloth – almost suffocating in their weight. With a creak of the wheels, the cart drove off and she kicked inside the bag to free herself. Before she succeeded, she was dragged into an inner courtyard. Two men cut open the bag and Josephine emerged,

4

wide-eyed, angry and scared. She looked first at the men and then at an old face that appeared from behind them.

"Welcome to Brienne," the old man said. "You may call me Master. You are fortunate – very fortunate. You have been chosen for training. A part of the new elite, the *crème de la crème.*"

He helped her up by the chin while the two men held onto her. She craned her neck toward an open doorway to see her new surroundings. She saw that other girls and boys near her age were in training, sparring and grappling with one another. They stopped to look at the unkempt girl in her blood-stained clothes, but Josephine was too ordinary and too scared to express any embarrassment at her appearance. She tried to break free but the men tightened their grip.

"If you do not cooperate," the old man said, "we will put you back in the bag. Hmm?"

She was led to a room where she cried tears of anxiety when they stripped her, bathed her, and shaved her head bald. The first new clothes she could remember was a cotton white cloak and she put it on. The first food she ate in days was beef stew with lots of potatoes and onions. She ate greedily, and then could not help but fall asleep. When she drifted off, she thought of her mother and cried herself to sleep.

The old teacher woke her with a splash of cold water in the face. She startled awake for it was still what some called "the crack of dark" and the man seemed more spirit than flesh.

"You didn't know I was here?" he asked.

She didn't answer and blinked her eyes to clear them.

"What would keep me from slitting your throat? Or worse. I could lock you in a box and bury you alive!"

She looked at him with fear for she was still quite young for such talk. He knocked twice on the stone floor with a cane and the same two men from before entered, carrying a box just her size.

She scrambled away from them but they caught her. She screamed and fought and kicked as they forced her into the box, closed the lid, and nailed it.

She screamed in terror and the two men left. The old man bent down over the box.

"Sssh, now," he said. "Calm yourself."

She ignored him and screamed again. She would've pulled her hair out if she had any. The old man lay down beside the box and put a hand on it.

"Remember, you have been chosen," he said to her. "Remember, you are only your actions. You are what you do, not what you think. Your actions should never betray your true feelings."

She was left there for a day. She banged and cried and defecated on herself. She was insane with fear. The next morning, they came again. When she thought it was over, they carried her out. She swayed in the box when they moved it, and she finally spoke.

"Please let me out!" she cried. "Please! I can't breathe! I'll be good!"

They ignored her and carried the box outside, where the torture started anew. They lowered her into an open hole. She felt the box hit the dirt and then the shovels brought clunks and clomps of dirt down on the top of the box.

"Noooo!!!" she screamed. And she wailed and cried.

"There are worse things than death," said the old teacher. "Our mind can be our worst enemy. If we don't control our thoughts, death can be a happy release."

"Please!" she begged from the depths of her soul. She was exhausted and felt the darkness. *Mercy. Mercy.* Yet none was given. In her state of mind, she was delirious and didn't realize that they had lowered her only a foot deep. And they had loosened the nails with each of her cries for help.

They shoveled the last bit of dirt over the box. In a moment of her utter collapse and quiet, the old man spoke his last words to her.

"Dig yourself out, girl," said the old teacher. "Or die. It is your choice."

She banged her head on the lid. She would kill herself if she could. It was better than the reality. Better than living. With the burial complete, the old man shooed away the workers and sat nearby. He picked a small flower with yellow petals and admired it.

Josephine was in a place she had never been. Dark, trapped, and alone, it was a torment of the mind. A battle of wills within her soul. She cried herself to exhaustion. Her breathing slowed and she saw light where there was none. She thought of her mother, her sisters and brothers, the village. She took some solace in knowing she would join them soon. She missed her mother. She missed everything that was.

She heard voices in her thoughts, and it was love and a beckoning to be calm; she lost track of time. And in one last moment of cold, hopeful observation, one self told the other that it wouldn't hurt anything to move her legs and her arms and push up against the lid. She did so, but nothing happened. She gained strength in her determination to perform one last act, one final effort, and she pushed again.

When the lid gave some and dirt seeped through, her psyche reunited and swelled with surprise. Hope could be a dangerous thing, but she felt the energy of it enter the box with her. She pushed and moved and banged until the lid gave some more.

When it gave, she inched it aside and dirt fell in. She wiped it from her eyes and spit it from her mouth. She saw a shaft of light peaking through the soil and she reached a hand toward it. Her hand pushed through and when she moved more dirt, more light came. Excited and frantic, she used both hands to claw away the dirt. She maneuvered her head above the ground and the rest of her body soon followed.

She sucked the air in and looked around. She had been buried in a beautiful garden hidden among old oak trees with long curved limbs that touched the ground and lush bushes full of ornamental berries. In the distance she could see workers in the field bent over and unaware of her. She turned to the old man who had stayed where he was and waited her out.

"You have passed the test," he said. When he smiled, she looked at him with fury and contempt.

7

"I hate you," she said. "I will kill you."

The girl spit dirt out of her mouth and toward the old man. If she still had the knife she used to kill the English soldier she would've thrown herself at him and stabbed the life from him.

"I see what he saw," the old man said with admiration. "You have unpolished strength. Hate, for example, can be a strength. It can be useful in many ways, as long as you are the master of it."

"I won't listen to you," she said. "I hate you and this place. I want to go home."

"Aah, well, this is your home," the old man answered. "This will be your home for many years."

"I'll run away."

"We will find you."

"I'll keep running."

"You won't get far without feet," he said. "And then you will have no further use to us."

Her chest heaved with emotion and she clenched her fists.

"You can always do more than you think," he said. "Your thoughts and emotions can betray you. This box represents a prison of your own making. Once you came to terms with your real situation, that you are both creation and destruction, you chose creation. You chose to control your own destruction."

"I don't care what you mean," she spit out. "You can't keep me here."

"And where would you go?"

"Anywhere!" she said. "Anyplace but here."

"And do what? Become a beggar, a whore? Someone's personal servant? Yes, that sounds much better."

The old man rose to his feet.

"Defiance," he said. "That's good. But recklessness? We will try to rid you of that."

The two men returned and Josephine was led back to the citadel. She was just one of several others in the same predicament. Orphans, throwaways, refugees. For some days after, Josephine was caught in a psychological drama. She was not the same person buried in the box as the one who came out. She had been snatched from her normalcy and thrown into something else, somewhere else. She was in a state of not fearing death but also not caring to live. Her fears had been cornered in the far reaches of her brain, but they still fought for recognition. This new world was foreign to her, and for all she knew, it also wouldn't last. It was during this stage of fragility that they begun to rebuild her.

"I want you to jump from here to there," the Master pointed with his stick. The ledge was six feet from the floor and covered with the grit of dust and decay. Young Josephine was gagged with a ball of cloth and had her hands tied in front of her. She looked at the height and looked at the Master and shook her head no.

When the blow came, it hit her back with such force that she felt it for days. Before the next blow, she jumped and pulled her way to the ledge. She was made to do this over and over until she could spring from her feet to the top of the ledge with ease.

The old man looked on and nodded his approval.

Josephine's days blurred into one another and her time asleep was the only time she was not directed, molded, and made to become a weapon. She was blindfolded and made to stand on a post. If she swayed too far one way, she fell and was beaten. Sticks poked her until she bruised. Whips slashed her until they left scars. They did this for hours over many days until she could hear the whip before it came. She could tell when someone's body weight shifted or a slight change in the air flow meant movement. She knew when the stick or a whip was coming toward her. She could move without falling and balance on one foot. She learned to catch the whip and to deflect the stick. They turned it into a game, giving her a whip to counter the blows. Even without sight, she turned the abuse on her abusers until they could strike her no more without receiving a lashing of their own.

The Master remained quiet but he was impressed. The girl was strong in spirit. If the men were doing too much, he motioned them to stop. If they were doing too little, he motioned them to do more. Josephine adapted and didn't break, and he knew this one was going to be something special.

As time passed, Josephine took to the regimented schedule. She was the first up and the last down. She learned quickly from her mistakes. She was a low maintenance recruit. She ate what was presented, kept her tongue, and mostly kept to herself. She could sit alone in the dark and remain still for hours, ignoring the sounds that bounced off the great stone walls around her. Mind and body blended and she was becoming a force.

While the wars continued and the empire grew, students became warriors and graduated. Each new crop was sent out to do their duty for the General. Some were sent to Egypt and fell in the desert sands. Others were left in Italy to guard the new empire. Some were sent on missions to the far reaches of the surrounding kingdoms, to bring back news and information, or to apply their talents in assassinations. So impressed was the General with the corps, that he kept sending resources to the citadel and the Master kept breaking and building them.

In a few years, Josephine rose to the top of her class. She was fast and agile. Her punches and kicks were almost faster than the eye, and her frame put on weight that gave her strength. She became a teenager in the citadel without the usual distractions. There was no dancing or songs or cake. No pretty dresses and parties, though every now and then the young warriors would notice each other in ways that led to inevitable youthful indiscretions. The Master was wise to this and kept the male and female recruits separated while increasing the level of barbaric training. Sometimes Josephine had her ears plugged with wax or her feet and hands were bound. Or the more common method of being blindfolded and gagged. At least one of her faculties was injured or stimulated so that her other senses were forced to compensate. In this manner, they molded her. When she reached sixteen, they tattooed the back of her neck with Napoleon's personal symbol: a honeybee over the letter "N".

Josephine was young when they received her, and when the Master recognized her strength of mind, he subjected her to more than the other orphans. With guns, swords, arrows, whips, and rope, they beat the girl out of her until the tears and losses were a faint memory in the woman warrior she became. She grew not only in stature and beauty but also in ability until she could best all of the females and most of the young males in her group.

One day, she sparred with a young man much like her – a vagabond picked up and broken into shape with the rest of them. They dueled until they cut each other. Where his weight and strength would overtake her while wrestling, her agility and skill would save her from being pinned. When he used fists, she used her feet and, before long, they were winded and at a draw. She finally bested him by ducking a wild swing, sweeping his legs out from under him, and putting a knife to his throat.

The Master told her to leave a mark so he would remember. She looked at the fellow teen and thought about doing it. But she was satisfied with the outcome and saw no need in scarring him. When she refused, she twirled the knife, stood up, and put it away. The Master look at his two henchmen and they came forward to make her comply. She responded by removing and casting the knife at the first, cutting his earlobe away. He yelled in pain.

"It is only a mark," she said.

The recruits were startled and awed that one of their own would dare to act against the Master. The man felt his bloody ear and he and his partner were angry with wounded pride. They pulled their own knives and moved to kill the upstart young woman when the Master raised his hand and stopped them.

This wasn't the first time a recruit had defied him. Only the best ever did. Only the ones who had reached that rare level of surety and willingness. He knew the time had come when the fledgling had outgrown the nest and, instead of offering condemnation, he smiled.

The final test for the recruits was designed for immersion with the enemy and the potential for death. So it was that each recruit was given oatmeal with opium. Some ate heartily and hit their heads on their bowls when the drug took its quick effect. Josephine, however, had been trained too well. She knew by the care with which the meal was served, the way the old teacher loitered nearby, and the unusual quiet, that something was different. She allowed herself to be drugged. She had come too far and had experienced too much, and she knew this last obstacle was not to kill her but to give her the way out.

When she awoke, she lay in a field of mud littered with bloated bodies and bad water and flies and scavengers. It brought back ugly memories and she scrambled to her feet. But the memories could not compete with the rituals of training. She knew the first thing was to find a weapon, but none were found. She did not know where she was, although some of the dead wore the yellow and red of the Spaniards. *Food, water, and a horse*, she told herself.

She ran to the woods and felt no fear. She plucked wild berries and drank from a stream. By nightfall, she had removed herself some miles from her starting point, using the sky for her guide home. She found a hamlet by its candlelight in the windows. She went to the barn and ate from the food left for the horses. She drank water from an unattended well. She climbed a nearby tree, tied herself to the trunk, and slept rather soundly on her first night out.

She was awoken by voices in the morning. When she peered down from her perch, she saw a man and a boy riding in a cart full of wheat. She was able to carefully slip down from the tree and conceal herself in the bales of wheat straw without notice. Judging from the location of the sun, Josephine knew she was south of the citadel and she was pleased that the cart was heading in the right general direction.

The man and boy rode for many hours and Josephine listened to their language and peered at the sky from her concealed place. She noticed the birds aflutter, the occasional tree that offered shade, and the dragonflies and bees that darted from place to place. She was a stranger in a strange land but she felt peaceful and unafraid. She felt free.

The cart left the dirt road and pulled into a small village with cobblestone streets. Josephine came out of the wheat and stepped down from the cart. She stole a shawl from a post and tied it around her head and shoulders in an attempt to blend in without being noticed. She did not speak the language and could not read the signs, though she observed a great deal of activity. An open market was active with a butcher selling slabs of meat and old women grilling bits of it over flames, a flower peddler selling fresh bouquets, vegetables of all types and colors being produced, and a large block of some kind of sweet seed paste that was chopped into small pieces for the children.

She noticed a crowd gathered at one side of the street and approached to observe. A small, portly man stood in the back of his wagon with one hand raised to the sky and another holding a small brown bottle.

"The secret elixir of the ancient world!" he boasted in the local language. "And now, for just a fraction of what you would pay to visit a physician, you'll have a medicine for your maladies right in your own home!"

The crowd was curious and listened for more. Josephine was also curious but for a different reason. She detected an inescapable French accent in the man's words. The man promised immediate cures from the contents of the bottle. Josephine decided it was the Spanish tongue he practiced, and he did it with good results. When he had sold all his bottles, he gave his horse a carrot, closed up his wagon, and rode away.

When night fell, the man pulled into a field and tethered the horse to a tree. He built a small fire for his camp and laid out his cooking utensils. While he was roasting potatoes, Josephine appeared and made herself known to him.

"My God, you scared the devil out of me!" the man exclaimed in French, before gaining his composure and settling back into Spanish. "From where did you appear?"

"I am heading to the mother country," she replied in French. "Would you allow me to travel with you?"

The man looked at her, puzzled at first, then laughed. "Sure, sure!" he answered in French. "It is not often that a man meets a fellow citizen in a land of barbarians. Come and share the fire."

Josephine squatted in front of the fire. She was not afraid of the man whose weapon was mostly his tongue and the girth of his waist.

"What you sold those people," she asked, "does it work?"

"For some, yes," he answered. "I only give them what they are waiting for."

"What is that?" she asked.

"Unseeable hope. It is what all wise men sell and what many thirst for."

"And you?" he asked. "What brought you to this land?"

Josephine did not know how to explain the unexplainable but she decided to try.

"I am trained to kill," she said, and the man almost spilled the hot potatoes.

"Yes, we seem to have plenty of those around about," he replied. "But you, why, you are just a girl. Why would you find yourself in this line of work?"

Josephine was stumped again about the best answer, but the man interrupted before she could speak.

"Aah, your fortune," he said. "Allow me to tell you your fortune. It may answer questions that both of us have."

She complied with a nod.

"There are many methods for doing this," he said, "but I believe that each person must be read in their own specific way."

He took her hand and held it. Her hand was smaller than his was but not delicate. He turned it over and looked at the creases in her palm and fingers. He wiped away some dirt for a better view and grunted to himself. He asked to see her tongue and she stuck it out. He examined it closely until she could smell his breath on her cheek.

"You are healthy and your lines run long," he said. "I see you as being alive for many years."

She had not thought of herself being an old woman someday. She had rarely considered her future beyond leaving the citadel and serving the General. None of her relatives had reached the status of being considered *old*. It was foreign and unexpected to her, so she immediately thought the man a fraud.

"I see you doubt my words," the man said. "Let us have a cup of plum wine."

He poured the wine from a corked bottle made of greenish-colored glass. He handed it to her and poured a cup for himself. Josephine smelled it and could smell both the aroma of the fruit and the fermentation. The taste was not entirely an unwelcomed flavor. The man watched her drink and after two more sips of the wine, he asked for the cup.

He took the cup and placed it on a tin dish. He then overturned the cup and spilled the bit of wine and sediment into the dish. He placed the dish over the fire and watched as the wine evaporated. When all that was left was the sediment, he motioned for Josephine to look closely.

"Aah, you see there," said the man. Josephine peered down over the sediment.

"I see the horse's head," he said, and he pointed with his pinky. Josephine looked intently, and with a little imagination, she could see the horse's head.

"And there," he pointed to another group of specks, "is the raven."

She inspected the sediment again and whether from the man's suggestion or her own thoughts, she saw a bird. She sat back and smiled for the first time.

"How much do people pay you for this entertainment?" she asked her new companion.

"No, no," he protested, "this is not entertainment. True, I may stretch my perception of things a time or two, but only if the sediments are few or if the person is inebriated. For you, it is only what the great mystery tells me," he continued.

"And what is that?" she asked.

"You have hidden strength, and you will use that strength many times during your life," he answered. "But there has also been great loss, and I don't believe you have seen the end of such calamity."

"You say things that can be interpreted in many ways," she said. "Perhaps I should give up my path and become a fortune teller myself."

"Mademoiselle," he answered, "you are hurting my feelings. Yes, on special occasion, I read and interpret in more than one way. But what is shown here has nothing to do with me. It is very clear to see. Your path in both body and spirit is not an ordinary one. But let us rest on it. I perceive that you must weigh my words, and I am confident that you will not beat and rob me in the middle of the night. I shall turn in, so I offer you the comforts of my camp and a pleasant *adieu*."

The man fed a couple of branches to the fire, crawled into his bedroll, and pulled the covers up. Josephine thought on her future and scoffed at interpreting her destiny by the creases of her tongue or the waste of the wine. But the seeds were planted and she looked at the ravens in the trees and other natural wonders differently from that point forward.

It took three days for Josephine to reach the citadel. What was to be the final test of the recruits turned into an altogether pleasant adventure for her. She would have to lie about the hardships encountered for concern of being put to another test. The fortune telling man was one of the first outsiders she had spoken to in many years and he shared his wisdom and ways of the world with her. He had offered enlightenment and humor as well as the promise of a bed and another reading if she ventured near his homestead in the winter.

Other recruits were not so fortunate as Josephine, or they took their newfound freedom for an opportunity to go their own way. Of the forty sent out, twenty-nine returned. The Master was not moved by the numbers; fate had culled the group. The odds fell in his favor on the number that returned and he had confidence in those he would be sending to the General.

When their graduation day came, Josephine was recognized for leading her class of recruits – an honor that did not sit well with some of her male counterparts, yet none were bold enough to question her or the Master. When they stood aligned in three rows, their old teacher gave his last testament to them.

"Some of you will be doing independent duty for the Empire," he said, "in places only you will ever see. Some of you will work in teams with your brothers and sisters. Your assignments will come quickly, with little notice, and without choice. Do you understand?"

"Yes, Master," they answered.

"You have everything to ensure your success. You have learned skills, you have weapons, and you have strength. Yet others will have them too. The one thing that makes you different, makes you more than most, is your mantra. You must remember your mantra."

"Yes, Master."

"Without it, you are a brute weapon with no purpose. You lose the strength of your soul, wherein lies hidden the real key to your power. Be ever mindful of it. It is an internal strength that is beyond the reach of any person. Now, repeat your mantra."

"I am the power.
My life is my own, my methods answer to no one.

I am the power.
I bring light to the dark, order to chaos, and fear to the fearless.

I am the power."

"Again," he said.

"I am the power.
My life is my own, my methods answer to no one.

I am the power.
I bring light to the dark, order to chaos, and fear to the fearless.

I am the power."

"Again," the teacher demanded. And the new class of France's best kept secret killers were ready.

Assignments were given and the warriors dispersed to make ready for departure. As Josephine prepared to leave, the old Master visited her. His two henchmen put a wooden box down in front of her, glanced at her with menace, and walked away. On the lid were the letters "LL" carved in italics.

"Open it," he said.

She dropped to her knees and did so. The first thing she saw was a mask that seemed to look back at her. She put it on and it covered her eyes, her cheeks, and the ridge of her nose. It had the same exposed-bone motif she remembered seeing as a little girl. It fit around her easily and molded to her skin. The teacher handed her a mirror and she looked at herself.

"We French must find the fashionable flair even in our tools of death," the teacher said and smiled.

She removed the mask and lay it aside. She brought the uniform up to her chest with both hands. It was the color of black pearl and the cloth shimmered when she moved it.

"I trust it is your size," he said. "We do not have many graduating women candidates, and only one who had the skill and strength to wear this particular piece."

The Master momentarily looked pained, and Josephine wondered if this was the uniform of the warrior she first laid eyes on as a girl.

"Our seamstress added silk for your comfort," continued the Master. "The rest is the strongest material in the empire."

Next were ceramic pieces of armor and footwear all of the same color and expected to deflect the blows of most swords and bullets. They had been formed to slip securely into pockets of the uniform and meld to the cloth, yet not to hinder her fighting ability. With the uniform on and the ceramic plates in place, Josephine looked more than her normal size. And she looked intimidating.

In the bottom of the box was a fake compartment lined in red velvet. She removed it and her eyes widened on seeing the weapons that would enhance her killing ability.

First were two pistols.

"These come from Gribeauval himself," said the old teacher. "Lightweight and accurate to a hundred yards. Do not lose them. You are the only one who has such a pair."

Next were daggers; black with rimmed handles for throwing and seven inches of razor-sharp death. Then, two swords in the samurai style; black handles wrapped and bonded with heat. She pulled one from its sheath, surprised at its lightness.

"These were specially imported," said the old teacher. "Forged day and night in the shadow of Nara. Smuggled out by Dutch traders. Probably the only dark swords in Europe. You will break before they do."

She stood and unsheathed the other sword. She ran both of them through the air. They were surprisingly light and agile, curving and lighter than the European cutlass, but just as deadly.

She twirled the swords in the air in a bold and acrobatic measure. She became one with the blades as they crossed and clanged and then she brought them down on each side of the teacher's head. She breathed through the moment and her chest heaved when she stared at him. She could take his head for the abuses he had wrought on her. But he knew she wouldn't. He smiled and bowed his head.

"*Lady Libertè*," he said.

2 THE GRAND ILLUSION

The citadel took on a brown hue in the early morning sun. The inner courtyard remained empty where Josephine and her brethren usually trained. The brothers and sisters of this graduating class of warriors sat at a long table for a final breakfast of coffee, hot oatmeal and croissants, soft butter, jam, and warm honey. Forks and knives were the only sound to puncture the otherwise quiet morning.

Josephine was assigned to the grand army with six of her classmates. She memorized the map and instructions given to her and handed them to the only other female of the group. They were to head east toward Moscow, where the old capital of the Russians had been taken by Napoleon and now the army was stretched thin trying to hold onto it. There were no tears and no goodbyes as the newly minted warriors nodded to the Master and dispersed.

Talking was not part of the warrior's repertoire. They did not share their excitements with one another over assignments, or the chance to finally do battle. Other mannerisms betrayed their enthusiasm; the way they rode their horses, cleaned their weapons, practiced their movements, and repeated their mantra.

The young warriors rode for weeks together, taking in their newfound freedoms with the zeal to prove themselves. Josephine tended to stay out in front, for she was the unspoken leader. The young males were pent up wanting action and more prone to drive their horses beyond their ability. They began to question Josephine for her prudence, and for simply being a woman. Josephine expected it and ignored most of the inquisitions. Her focus was fixed on the assignment and she gave little time to meaningless distractions.

When they crossed into Russia, the first lesson of the new reality was waiting for them. The farther they traveled, the colder it became and snow covered every feature of the landscape. Many of their fallen French comrades had been heaped together in great piles and burned to ashes. Others lay frozen in their final resting place in various stages of raising their hands to the heavens and having been feasted on by the birds and beasts of the fields. The Russians left empty cabins, dead livestock, and poisoned wells in a trail behind them, leaving no material goods for the invading French. They occasionally took shots at Josephine and her brethren from faraway trees and earthen banks. When Josephine and her brethren chased them, the Russians sped away on their horses, only to return and repeat the harassment. This continued for some time and soon the young warriors had drained the resources they'd brought with them.

Josephine was forced to drink melted snow and take food from where she could get it. Together they chased wolves away from the carcass of a deer and roasted it for themselves. By the time they made it to Moscow, each had lost more than weight. They had lost the exhilaration of ignorance and youth for being at war.

They found their army dejected and unprepared for the bitter climate and the lack of supplies and bounty in the old Russian city. Despondency had taken hold of Napoleon's foot soldiers. Josephine was one of the first elite guards the soldiers had seen. They sized her up on her pretty horse, with her fancy uniform and her special weapons. Instead of saluting the glory of France, they spit on the ground.

"Why you come here?" one soldier asked. "There's no war. No trophies to be had. Only more mouths to feed. If you brought no food, then go home."

She had never seen the army like this, never known it to be defeated. During the years of training, they were told how close France was to ruling the civilized world. Now many of the soldiers were huddled together around open fires, shivering against the cold, drinking whatever brought warmth and forgetfulness. She could hardly believe it. She had never questioned the inevitable glory of the man who had chosen her that day. Yet she knew better than to believe everything she was told. *Foolish girl,* she told herself. Perhaps the Master himself did not know how bad things were. Nevertheless, she would not stand by and do nothing.

She put her skills to work. While her brethren took up positions to guard the army, she patrolled the Kremlin at night and brought the army what it required. She harvested stray animals for food; dogs, cats, rabbits, and birds. In her nightly ritual, she rode up to the many fires and dropped her bounty for the soldiers. Instead of thanking her, they mocked her.

"That's a fine horse," one said. "We could eat for a week on such a beast."

"Make it easy on yourself," another said. "Just bring us some of that Russian vodka and forget the food."

They laughed and Josephine ignored their words. The Russians, however, saw no humor in the imposing warriors on their horses, fully cloaked in the dark. Josephine and her warrior sister rode together through the streets and into the alleyways and backyard gardens. They'd take a chicken or a goose if there was more than one. A dog made the mistake of jumping at her sister's horse and it became dinner. The Russians whispered among themselves about a pair of twin demons in the night who would come from the west and kill them and steal their children. They looked out their windows in the moonlight and feared seeing the demonic apparitions on horseback. Many began to leave the carcass of a rabbit or a raccoon on the doorstep, hoping to be passed over.

Josephine was not kind to such make-believe and bedtime stories. She remembered some that her mother had told her, yet her experience was to fear what she could see, not the stories of the imagination. Man was more than capable of enough evil; to conjure up the acts of witches and ghosts was childish. Yes, this "demon" would surely kill them if necessary for the Empire, but she was no threat to them or their children – only their dog, or a stray cat, or the gander that honked and hissed too loudly.

For three months, Josephine helped to feed her Frenchmen. Her brothers and sisters found themselves little to do in the way of what they had expected. The Russian army had abandoned Moscow to the winter and the invaders, leaving the warriors with no real action or resources and Napoleon in a frozen standstill.

Some of the soldiers took their frustration out on the Russian people, and more than once Josephine found herself between her compatriots and the local inhabitants. She would not abuse the innocents of the war. She would not do what was done to her. One evening she patrolled alone, and she came across one of her brethren having his way with a Russian woman. She stopped her horse to observe. Under normal circumstances, Josephine – regaled in her uniform with her weapons and her veil – would invoke caution in any would-be sightseers. But this brother knew her, and he took license with their familiarity.

"Keep to your own business," he hissed at her. Josephine did not move and the woman looked at her, beckoning for help.

"Leave the woman alone," Josephine said imperiously. "You do us great dishonor with your actions."

The warrior cast the woman aside.

"The Master's pet again," he said. "You don't scare me. You think you're above us and can tell the rest of us what to do."

Josephine dismounted and approached.

"You take leave of your senses, brother," Josephine said. "Come with me and I will find you a place to rest."

The young warrior reached for his weapon.

With swiftness, Josephine pulled her dagger out and cast it freely toward the young man. It plunged into the flesh of his hand and he screamed in pain. With a swift kick, Josephine dropped him to the ground and stood over him. Her hands were full providing for the needs of an army that didn't want to be there, the desire of some of her brethren to try out their skills in the wrong way, and the pressing Russian winter. She had no time for the insolence of one of her own.

She put her boot on his neck.

"Next time you break our code, I will remove your hand," she said.

"You are right, sister," he said. "I lost my way. Forgive me."

She extracted the dagger and the young warrior howled again.

"Go and tend to your wound," Josephine said. "I will come in a moment."

He did as requested and pulled himself up on his horse, then left. The Russian woman stared at Josephine, and spoke her thankfulness but Josephine did not understand. Josephine wiped the dagger off in the snow, sheathed it, and remounted. The woman backed away passively, crossing herself from right to left, without turning her back on her dark savior.

While the winter raged, the need for warmth and heat increased. The sun was rarely seen in the gray skies over Moscow and the men were succumbing to physical and mental exhaustion. One evening, a soldier was detached from the General's staff to deliver a message to the young warriors. At the stated time, they were to present themselves in Red Square and wait. They complied without hesitation, not knowing what the outcome was to be.

Josephine was the first to see him approaching. By the time Napoleon rode up with his attachment, she could see he was a different man. Still strong and forceful for his size, still an unnatural selection of courage and honor contained in a frame of Romanesque proportions – but he looked tired with the weight of the Empire carried firmly on his shoulders. When he dismounted, Josephine and her compatriots were startled; they dismounted immediately.

They had not seen the General in many years. Some of her brother and sister warriors had never seen him. Napoleon gazed on each of them. His hat was snug on his head and he warmed one hand inside the opening of his shirt. He walked a line in front of them as they stood solid and straight. He stopped momentarily in front of Josephine, then continued on. *Did he remember her?*

"Did you know the Master was my own teacher?" he began. "A Corsican. I trust he was not too gentle with you?" Napoleon managed a slight smile while he looked them over. Josephine was somewhat in awe of him. Despite the circumstances, he was still the man who changed her life forever, and she had learned from the teacher about his exploits.

"I must say, I am very impressed at your appearance. I had hoped we would have more action for you at this point, but it seems our adversaries have simply vanished. Such is war. One must always prepare and expect the unexpected."

Napoleon used a handkerchief to dab at his nose, dripping from the cold.

"Soon enough there will be more to do. That I can promise you. And then each of you will have your own stories to tell. Your own beginnings in the art of making war. And why is this? Because we are French, brothers and sisters. We do what others are unwilling to do. Only our readiness to reach for greatness has led us here to the capital of our enemy."

"Take heart, brethren," he continued. "I know that all you may remember is the cold and the suffering of this land. What I will remember is the boldness of our acts – of raising our voices in the land of the tsars. What exhilaration. So many live their whole lives for so little, without ever reaching their true destinies. And yet you were willing to venture into the unknown; into the lands forbidden by only our own fears. For that, I salute you."

"But now, brothers and sisters, we are under siege on all sides of our homeland. Why? Because we dare to do more. The liberties and freedoms of the French Revolution have never been under more threat. Even from enemies within. So remain strong, my young warriors, and powerful for the cause. War and rumors of war will be the high price we pay for the luxury of liberty across the whole of Europe."

He looked across Red Square, his breath misting in the cold air.

"Let us turn our attention to new horizons. Let us leave this place of cold and desolation. There is nothing more we can do for these people here, and our countrymen now call us home."

Napoleon saluted and left, followed by his entourage. He rode away that night for Paris, leaving most of his army behind – as well as the dreams and broken promises of many citizens who gave all for so little.

When the retreat began, Josephine and her brethren took up positions at the rear. Snow was heavy on the ground and the army left the city with only a few prized treasures and the clothes on their back. There was no fighting; the Russians were happy to see them leave. Josephine and the others followed behind, and the long trail of the occupiers was soon obscured in a blanket of snow.

For several days, the army marched. Their fight was against the elements. The ice and the snow and the freezing temperatures were killing the men faster than any Russian, English, Italian, or Egyptian ever had. As the grand army marched on, the young warriors drove their horses along the ridges

26

and hills. They used the advantage of height to monitor the movements of their army and any human predators. The French pressed forward to the warmth of their Mediterranean homeland. To the "unseen hope", the fortune teller had told her. Those without the strength to continue lay down with their dreams and froze to death.

Josephine watched and waited for any threats that might appear but there was nothing she could do about the weather. She spent the hours counting the corpses that were quickly buried and forgotten by the snow. She kept her emotions in check and concentrated on the objective at hand. She had not yet risen to the level of questioning a grand design of putting so many troops and resources so far away, but the cold in her bones and the indeterminable benefit of the occupation weighed on her as much as it did her compatriots.

"What are we doing here?" one warrior asked Josephine. "This is madness."

Josephine didn't know how to answer, for thoughts of treason were never shared and never spoken aloud. She was troubled by the situation but not enough for an act of sedition. Not just yet. She had known needless destruction and the pain it brought. Death was death no matter what colors were worn or banners were raised; and if it came a little quicker from an unfavorable outcome, one just dealt with it.

"I've seen worse," she said.

"Have you?" another young warrior said. He pulled his horse up to face Josephine.

"We'll be lucky if we can die in our own land for that little bastard."

"It is not for us to decide," she answered. "We do our duty and be proud of it."

"Aah, Josephine," he replied and sneered sarcastically. "Did you not forget your own identity? How is it that so few seem to profit from this fight for liberty? I sit frozen in my saddle wielding a sword while another lies in bed wielding his cock with his face buried in tits! I think I would rather trade places." He bent closer to her, "If I were to strike the General down, wouldn't we be better off?"

"You speak like a foreigner!" cried another warrior, the one wounded by Josephine. "You forget your honor, and your place!" He looked to Josephine for confirmation.

"Do I?" said the defiant one. "I was not aware I had given up so much, for so little."

"The Master might as well have taken your tongue!" said the other female warrior.

"On the contrary, he seems to have taken all of yours!" he replied.

"Stop!" said Josephine. She looked at the questioning warrior. "You may be right. But save your words for another day, brother. Our current enemy approaches."

From the edge of the woods, a group of Russians on horseback entered the field. These were the first they had seen in the many days of retreat.

"Cossacks!" said one of the warriors. They unsheathed their swords.

When the first group of Cossacks crossed the field, a second group soon followed, tipping the scales.

"There are too many, brothers and sisters," said Josephine. "Let us wait for them to take rest and then we will gain the upper hand."

The errant brother donned his mask. "By that time, they will be feasting on our fellow soldiers, sister. I tell you what. I shall claim five, if you can manage your one. If I fail, you may give your regards from one little bastard to another."

Before Josephine could issue him restraint, the warrior broke from the group. And as the *esprit de corps* obliged them to do so, Josephine and the rest followed.

They bore down quickly on the Cossacks but without surprise. The Cossacks turned to face the invaders. The army of demons would have provoked fleshly fear in most, but the Cossacks were from the same hardened training. They set themselves tight in the saddle and raised their long rifles.

When they fired, it was the horses of three young warriors that fell to the ground. The Cossacks had learned; their bullets may break against the uniforms of these invaders, but their horses were big targets and bled quickly and easily. The warriors were catapulted from their saddles. Josephine escaped the initial barrage and remained on horseback. She unsheathed both her swords and headed into the fire.

The slaughter commenced.

Josephine rammed through the middle and relieved two Cossacks of their heads. Her French brothers and sister broke to the left and the right, cutting through the ranks until they had completely passed. The numbers had evened out when they crossed each other and turned for a second pass. Josephine heard laughter and set her eyes on a long-bearded Cossack with a bear-fur coat. He had dismounted and grabbed one of her downed brothers. With a twist and a tug, he tore the head from the torso with his bare hands. He lifted the trophy high for all to see and roared his delight.

Josephine bore down on him with the full force of her hatred and intensity. He saw her coming and beckoned her forward. He produced a chain from under the bear fur. When she rode closer, he swung it, hooked her arm and sword, and yanked her from the saddle. She tumbled to the ground. The bear man blocked a swing of her sword and pounced on top of her. He laughed while he squeezed her. She was in trouble but she had been in this situation before. Her hands searched for anything to grab. But the huge man was heavy and she felt the breath leaving her body.

Then a hand came over the top of the bear man's head, grabbing him by his woolly hair and jerking him up. A blade was placed at his throat.

"That's my sister, you animal," he said. Whether or not the Cossack understood the words, he felt the pain when the knife slit his throat. The bear man released her and grabbed at his throat. Her brother warrior wiggled her free, and she realized it was the one she had wounded in Moscow. With no time for gratitude, she retrieved a sword and pierced the bear man through. They turned from each other and continued the fight. The snow became speckled with blood and limbs and when the fighting was over, the French had taken the ground.

One of their seven had perished and they removed his armor and weapons as their custom dictated. They had taken numerous Cossacks but the high price for their one was still not felt high enough. Josephine recovered her horse and her weapons while another warrior stabbed angrily at the Cossacks on the ground.

"Just in case," he said.

"Josephine," a voice called.

The warriors gathered toward a wounded member when she collapsed to the snow. The only other female of the group. Josephine ran to her side and lifted her fallen comrade's head. She removed the veil and searched for the wound with her hands. She found it in the young warrior's side between her ceramic shields. The blood ran dark and Josephine feared for the outcome. Josephine took a flask and gave her water to sip. The face of the fallen female was as white as the snow around her.

"I am the power," she said.

"You are the power, sister," said Josephine, "and you fought bravely. No one will forget. I promise you."

The young warrior wanted to talk again but she couldn't. When she died, the others removed her shielding and her weapons and divided them among themselves. Josephine caressed her hair and could not hide a few tears while she held her. The one who impatiently led the charge pulled on her shoulder.

"Leave her," he said. "Your softness will get you killed."

"Your lust for glory will get us all killed, brother," she replied.

She glanced at him angrily, and then abruptly turned away.

When Josephine finally left her fallen sister, the remaining four took to their saddles and hurried to catch up with the rear of the army. As each day passed, Josephine and her brothers killed more skirmishers and would-be assassins. Yet the retreat was a disaster. The closer they came to France, the more soldiers fell victim to disease and the harshness of the winter elements that followed them from Russia. Josephine and her brothers fought valiantly to protect them, but there would be no recognition and no record of their achievements. Mother Nature would be the one collecting the honors.

One night, the wind died down and the snow fell soft and blue. Josephine recognized the beauty of it, the sincerity of it, even when death was always nearby and waiting. She and her remaining brothers camped on a ledge, careful not to draw attention with a fire, and watched the main road near the border crossing for signs of followers.

Two riders of unknown origin came up the road.

"I will take them," said a brother.

"No, I will," said Josephine.

She left the ledge and trotted her horse to the road. She stopped and waited. When the riders came closer, she unsheathed her swords.

"Who follows after the Grand Army?" she called out in French.

The riders stopped and did not answer. They did not flee and she would not yield the road. A brief flash of light and the gunshot punctured the night. Josephine blocked the shot with a whip of her blade.

While the horsemen deliberated their next move, she kicked her own horse into action. She rode from the left and then cut between them. She forced herself through the horses, knocking them off balance, and she slashed. She cut one across the chest and one across the back and the men fought to regain control of their horses and not fall from their saddles. She wheeled around and stopped. They turned to face her again and she brandished both swords parallel to the ground for the men to see. She appeared to be a long-haired demon intent on taking the rest of their blood. This time, they acquiesced and abandoned the road in a hurry.

Josephine did not give chase and the brothers came out onto the road.

"Don't let them go!" one said.

"Leave them!" she said. "By the time their wounds heal, the army as well as we will be back in Paris."

He looked crossly at her. "You would let many of our men fall while two of theirs yet live?"

"I had not the time to discuss their origins or their destination, brother," she answered. "But I would not bind all men to evil intention and save my sword for another day."

"If you have that day, sister," he grumbled.

With most of their supplies gone and the woods becoming less profitable, the young warriors were relieved to finally cross the French border. But times had changed since they last stepped foot on their own soil. Even their fellow Frenchmen were against them. Bedraggled soldiers were scattered by the wayside, begging for food, water, and medicine. Napoleon had raised his countrymen up only to bring them down to ruin. The country was now in a shambles and in that transitional period where old scores were settled and new alliances emerged. A secret messenger sent from the old Master caught up to them on the road.

"You can see the state of things with your own eyes," the messenger said. "The Master tells you not to return. Napoleon is overthrown."

The young warriors looked at each other.

"You see," said the impatient brother, "what did I tell you? What was it our sister and brother perished to preserve? Well, I go to make my own way in the world."

"You would leave us so quickly?" asked Josephine.

He rode up close to Josephine.

"Remember what I told you, sister," he said. "The world is a cold, hard place with little room for the nature of a woman." He kissed her hard on the lips, and she pushed him away.

"Follow me, brothers!" he laughed. "We are free!"

They all complied, although the one who Josephine wounded turned to her before leaving.

"Yours is the power, sister," he said.

"And yours, brother," she replied.

She watched him ride away with the others. Josephine, for the first time in her life, was on her own. She continued to the citadel alone. She found the grounds empty of students and ransacked, yet she knew; this place was the only place for the old Master. He would never leave it. She drew out a pistol and searched room to room before she found him. She was startled to see him, for someone had relieved him of his eyes.

He sat up, weak and dejected, but he knew her presence.

"You've returned to gloat at your old Master?"

Josephine felt compassion, pity, and anger. Her emotions were fertile ground for exacting revenge, but on who and for what real purpose she could not decide.

She put her pistol away.

"Are there any others?" she asked.

"All are gone," he replied sadly. "All is gone."

"Come," she said, "I will take you somewhere more safe."

"No," he replied. "My time is over. But you? Your time is just beginning. Take your freedom and go. Find a place your heart desires. Find something worth living for."

"I'll not leave you."

"Now you are the master," he jested. He lay down. "Go, and let me die with some dignity."

Emotions stirred in her and she mulled over the choices ahead of her.

"Where is the General?" she said.

"They took him to the harbor," he answered. "Do not go there. It would be an unnecessary sacrifice. You have more to give than these fools are worth."

The old Master breathed slowly. She watched him, observing the man that had raised her not as a child, but with weapons of war and little mercy. And she sympathized with his condition but was not happy with herself for doing so. Then she turned and left.

She raced for the harbor still unclear of what she should do if she found him. The walkway and open square were full of citizens racing around in states of agitation. Guns were shot in the air for celebration while others watched discreetly from doorways and windows. Some stared at her, for they had never seen a woman warrior. Others moved aside and paid her no attention. And then she saw him.

Napoleon had been taken in chains on board an English ship. The sails were set and a full attachment of English soldiers stood between her and the ship. The English Admiral Cockburn watched from the deck as he took ownership of the prized possession.

How could they do this? she thought to herself. *How could it end like this?* She wanted the arrogant Englishman to taste his own blood. She wanted the monarchists who had betrayed their own Frenchman to be publicly condemned. She wanted to save the man who saved her, and she thought her sacrifice would be worth it.

But she didn't move. Not today. She was not suicidal or stupid. This was a battle she would not win and damn if the old Master wasn't right again.

"For you is the glory!" she yelled. And Napoleon heard her above the fray. He turned to her from aboard the ship, removed his hat, and bowed to her. A smile and look of defiance crossed his face and he seemed to stand a little taller. He continued under guard across the deck until she could see him no more. Admiral Cockburn took notice of her and they both stared, one warrior to another.

"That's one of his guards," Cockburn said to a soldier near him. "Get after that devil and cut her down!"

A detachment of soldiers marched from the boat. Josephine weighed the odds of winning the encounter, then swallowed her pride. She turned back for the citadel and left the harbor.

The citadel was the one brutal place that had been more of a home than anywhere on the Earth. She entered for the last time and took up the body of the old master. She buried him on the grounds near the same place he had buried her. She removed her uniform and stored her tools of the trade in the box and donned the cloak of a common woman.

For several days, Paris burned. With the help of the English, the French greeted the return of their old, fat King and restored the monarchy. To show their faithfulness, eager French citizens sought out Napoleon's people and put them on the rack or sent them to the guillotine.

Josephine paid to board a ship for America. From the ship's deck, she hugged her horse and watched her homeland diminish, but she shed no tears. She was leaving no one behind. She was free to make her way or to succumb to circumstance.

For the first time in her life, she was free to simply be a woman.

3 LAND OF THE FREE

The moon hung low over the horizon and allowed the lamplighters along Pennsylvania Avenue to work a bit slower. The White House was already overflowing with guests when another horse and carriage arrived to unload its occupants.

Inside, a quartet of violinists played madly. An old-time dance was in progress and the room bulged with state leaders, powdered ladies, military elite, and dashing young cadets.

Amid the twirl, the movement, and the music, President James Madison entered from a side room with his wife Dolley. Those who saw them enter politely applauded. The President and his wife held hands and their eyes locked. Madison was the elder statesman, the author of independence. Although short in stature, he was a man among men in the room. But in this case, he was overshadowed by the blue eyes and fair skin of his charming hostess wife. She smiled grandly to him and gave a slight bow to the applause in the room. The dancing continued, stealing attention away from the President and First Lady.

Major John Singleton and his French bride, Josephine, found themselves in the center of the room. The Major looked the part of a dashing soldier; mid-twenties, dark hair, dark eyes, and recently minted from West Point. Although American born, he still hadn't quite shaken an English accent. He was already a veteran with the war begun two years earlier. It was duty and honor and the stars and stripes forever in his future, though concern had grown that 1814 would only bring more confrontation with the English in Canada and soon in Maryland and Virginia.

Josephine was every bit his equal and a contender with the army for his attention. She was one of the new Americans, an outcast from the European wars. She could draw a crowd with her looks alone, but it was the warrior's soul that had drawn the Major to her. She kept her past to herself and the Major did not know the full extent of her background; that she knew how to draw blood and lots of it. But through their sparring and bonding, he knew she was no ordinary woman, which made her all the more captivating.

They held their hands high with fingers locked, smiling devilishly at each other, matching each step, and ending with an affectionate embrace. He held her effortlessly in a dip, and placed his face near her bosom. When he brought her back up, an unspoken look of desire passed between them.

"The Major has done well for himself," the President said to his wife.

"As has she," Dolley answered with a coy smile.

Outside the city, a rider was nearing in full stride. He lashed a stirrup against his galloping horse. They streaked across a bridge and down a dirt road. He lost his hat, but he dared not to stop. The rider was young, and he was scared. He knew that the information he had could get him killed.

"Yaaaaaahhhh!!!" the young rider yelled at his horse.

His clothes were streaked with dust and sweat from the journey. He dug again into his mount's ribs and the horse responded, flailing for breath.

The dancing in the White House intensified with the passion of the music. The President and First Lady mingled while John and Josephine continued to garner their own audience. John slid his hand down her back as he supported her, raising her leg with his other hand and holding her thigh. Josephine closed her eyes and her chest heaved. The violinists played like there was no tomorrow.

Outside, the young rider glanced nervously over his shoulder. He wasn't going to make it – a shadow was closing in. He heard a *gunshot* and the messenger hugged the saddle, hunching down closer to the horse. He was scared but determined to make it.

A man kneeled next to a tree. He reloaded methodically. He raised the rifle, set the distance, and braced himself against the tree. From his point of view, he had only one more chance to get the rider. He *fired*.

The rider lurched forward from the impact of the bullet hitting his back. Blood dribbled from his mouth as he managed to stay in the saddle. The horse carried the wounded rider over a hill and out of sight.

When the dance ended, the President and First Lady bowed to each other and then to the crowd. John and Josephine stole a kiss and bowed as well. All clapped for the entertainment and for their good fortune.

Moments later, three war leaders mounted the stairs to the second floor. General Winder removed his hat and nervously ran a hand through his hair. He was in over his head and he knew it. He almost dropped the satchel of papers he carried.

Secretary of War Armstrong – short, fat, and pompous – followed close behind the General. Seeing a potted flowering plant on the way in, he picked the only stem in bloom, smelled it, and stuck it in his vest buttonhole. Rounding out the group, Secretary of State James Monroe was the most competent and the most assured of the three. Although in his fifties now, he still looked agile enough for battle. He had seen dire times during The Revolution; they had beaten the British once, and they could do it again. Already at the top of the stairs, he removed his riding gloves and waited for Armstrong and Winder.

Servants opened the doors and the three men entered the Presidential office. Oil lamps lit the grand room filled with books and papers, upholstered sofas, a large mahogany table, and an expansive window overlooking Pennsylvania Avenue.

President Madison was writing at his desk with a quill pen and didn't look up.

"Come in, gentlemen," he said. "Just finishing some papers."

The men looked nervously at each other and meandered about the room, admiring the paintings on the walls. Armstrong sat down and lit his pipe.

"Quite an evening of entertainment," he continued. "There now. I am just finishing our directives for the negotiating team in London. God knows we need to hear something soon before things get too far out of hand. If only old Ben Franklin were here to offer some wit and wisdom."

He looked at Monroe and placed the quill in its holder and closed the inkwell.

"Alright, General Winder. Let's have it."

General Winder came to the table and placed the dead rider's satchel on it. He carefully removed the bloodstained papers. With trembling hands, he unfolded a map and laid it out on the table.

President Madison moved to the table and looked at the map. Secretary of State Monroe ran his finger along the U.S. coastline, stopping at Chesapeake Bay. Secretary of War Armstrong got up and glanced quickly at the map, then sat back down in a chair near the table.

"The ships are anchored here," said General Winder. He cleared his throat and pointed to Baltimore Harbor on the map. "At least fourteen vessels. Two battle class frigates. We think it is Admiral Cockburn."

The General cleared his throat again, and continued. "There do seem to be some troops sent ashore. The rest of the Chesapeake is completely sealed off. We cannot get to the Navy left in the yard."

Madison and Monroe both looked at Winder with surprise. Armstrong inhaled his pipe.

"Barney's men are there now and ready to scuttle our fleet," added Winder. "If we don't want the British to have them."

"Good God," exclaimed Monroe. "You're mad!"

"What is the intent here, General?" President Madison demanded. "You wish to destroy the American Navy with nary a shot being fired?"

"Mr. President," he replied nervously.

"Where's our army, General?" Monroe interrupted.

"Most of our troops are still in Canada, Mr. Secretary," he answered. "I have been working with Secretary Armstrong to raise the state militias."

"The British know we are overextended," added Secretary Monroe. "And, I must say, unprepared!" He looked at Armstrong.

40

"Even Boston or New York did not merit this kind of interest from them," Secretary Monroe continued. "They are coming here to Washington."

Armstrong scoffed, grandly waving his pipe.

"That is preposterous," he declared. "There's no purpose to such an act."

"Then why would they sail into Baltimore and send men ashore when their navy can do enough from the sea?" demanded Monroe.

"I see plenty of purpose as well, Secretary Armstrong," the President interjected. "Why would they risk coming so far inland without taking the greatest prize possible? You know your history. Cut off the head, the rest will crumble."

"In the eyes of the world, Mr. President, Washington is still very much the backwater," Secretary Armstrong replied. "Dirty streets and livestock running loose. It's Baltimore they prize – the port and all of its possessions. These men are driven by greed, they want to line their pockets. They're not in it for childish adventures. The best Washington can offer them is reams of paper and a few crooked lawyers."

"You rest too much on your own opinions, sir," said Secretary Monroe.

Secretary Armstrong jumped out of his chair. "I have it under great authority--"

"Your authority is to prevent and prepare for war!" interrupted Secretary Monroe.

"Gentlemen!" shouted President Madison.

They stopped and took a deep breath.

"General Winder," asked the President, "what is the rest of your assessment?"

Winder paused and wiped his brow, clearing his throat once more.

"I agree with Secretary Monroe, to a point," he answered. "They will make a push for the Capitol. They'll send their army here but keep the navy in Baltimore."

"We've sent for all militia available," added Secretary Armstrong. "Baltimore has its entire army available but General Smith will not release them with the British blockading the harbor."

"Nor would I," answered the President. "We will ask the other states to send all able men, including their slaves."

"This is outlandish!" declared Secretary Armstrong. "We run the risk of creating mayhem out of this madness – exactly what the English would like! This is still very much in the realm of being a ruse to get us to overreact. Besides, militia are best employed at the last minute!"

"We have British forces in the Bay less than thirty miles from here!" Secretary Monroe countered heatedly. "They are not sightseeing. I would like to hear your reasoning for the delays in which you--"

"Mr. President, this is what they want!" Secretary Armstrong interrupted. "Harassment! Pandemonium! A slave rebellion. There are a half-million slaves in this country to incite!"

"Your inaction will see to that," Secretary Monroe challenged, glaring at Armstrong.

"Mr. President, I shall begin the defense of Washington immediately," said General Winder.

"Yes," answered President Madison.

"We'll need approval to move the militias across state boundaries," added the General.

"For God's sake, they have just finished Napoleon," exclaimed Armstrong. "The English are tired. They don't want to commit more men when only the threat of such would do considerably more."

Armstrong pointed a finger at General Winder. "They want us kept busy moving troops to and fro while they secure Canada."

"The Canadian front has nothing to do with this escalation," countered the General.

The President turned to his old friend, Secretary Monroe.

"Jemmy?" he said.

"Yes, Mr. President?"

"You met this Cockburn."

"I have, Mr. President."

"What kind of man is he?"

"Very English," answered Secretary Monroe. "Pompous and prone to opportunity. He will be a formidable foe. He has the Royal Navy at his disposal, and I imagine it is Wellington's troops he's brought with him."

He paused to remember more details. "He has written to me before. When General Washington was President. He was quite candid about repairing the breech between the colonies and the King by use of force. I would wager he intends to take Baltimore, but he will lay waste to our Capitol if he can."

President Madison looked alarmed.

"Old grievances die hard," said Secretary Monroe. "To go down in history as the man who retook the rebellious colonies? Men have been driven to do terrible things for much less."

"It is preposterous," said Secretary Armstrong.

"General Winder?" asked the President.

"We are not ready for a full-scale assault," answered the General.

President Madison looked out the window while he weighed all points of the discussion.

"I think it has been decided," the President said after a moment of reflection. "We are to receive nothing but outrage from the English. With our friends in France defeated, it has come to this. We are in a terrible position. I fear the British are in a vindictive mood. There's no more time to wait for political outcomes."

He turned to General Winder. "Continue your operations, General. Get every man that you can."

Then he turned to Secretary Armstrong. "Mr. Secretary, you'll open up the stockades. See to it that every horse, every cannon, every piece of ammunition is at General Winder's disposal."

The President turned back to General Winder. "Let the Baltimore regiment stay in Baltimore for now. I'll draw up orders for a general recruitment."

"Yes, sir," answered General Winder, who then turned and left the room.

"Mr. President," Secretary Monroe said, "allow me to take a horse and rider and go out toward the bay. Have a look around."

The President smiled. "You fancy yourself a young revolutionary again," the President said. "Miss the action, do you?"

"Those were the best days, Mr. President," replied Secretary Monroe with a smile of his own.

"Don't get yourself shot, Jemmy," said the President. "All I need is a dead secretary on my hands."

Monroe picked up his white gloves and turned to Secretary Armstrong. "Wish to accompany me and convince yourself?"

Armstrong dismissed the idea with a wave of his hand.

"As you wish," answered Secretary Monroe, and then left the room.

The President walked back to the window. Pennsylvania Avenue was fairly deserted; most of the guests had returned to their homes. The darkness was punctured only by the lamps and the slice of the moon not hidden behind clouds. He could discern an occasional pedestrian by the glow of lit tobacco and he caught a glimpse of the flag when the wind ruffled it. He saw his own reflection in the window and wondered how he had become so old so quickly.

4 THE FARM

Virginia was still fertile ground for romance and old revolutionaries. In the city of Alexandria, the former colonialists had built a prosperous city via agricultural production and government largesse. It's proximity to the capital made it prime real estate for the newly minted officers in the regular army, contractors looking to bid on government works, and the simple well-to-do wanting the country lifestyle within a stone's throw from Washington. Horse-drawn carts filled with sellers and goods kept the dirt roads active and the farmers busy but content. Cottage homes sprung up along the roads and on the perimeter of the forests, competing with the native fox and deer for space.

John stood in the middle of a horse-training ring he had cut out of pasture. When he wasn't at war, he fancied himself the Jeffersonian type. The gentleman farmer with the highest ambitions for Virginia and his new country. He held a saddle with all the intent of getting it on the horse in front of him. The black mare appeared to have no intention of letting him.

"Whoa, girl, whoa."

The horse backed away from him as he turned toward the laugh behind him.

With her long dark hair pulled back in a knot, Josephine sat on the fence and smiled at her husband. This regal French beauty was amused at the man who could tame her but not her horse.

"You're not helping," said John.

"She's playing with you," said Josephine, her English still betrayed by a French accent. "Show her who is in charge."

He tried to get the saddle on the horse and missed. When he fell, he received a mouth full of dirt and little sympathy. Josephine laughed at him again but this time jumped down to help.

"Let me try," she said.

He stood aside. Her demeanor was confident and assuring, and she coaxed the horse toward her with a wave of her hand.

"Take pity on him, sister," she said to the horse in French. The horse walked to Josephine and allowed her to put the saddle on.

"That's it. That's it. Good girl."

John watched and didn't know whether to feel ashamed or proud. She tied the saddle on and the horse was ready to ride.

"See," said Josephine, "you just have to know how to talk to a woman."

She handed the reins to John with a sly grin.

"You two are conspiring against me," he said. "I've not been gone that long that she forgets me."

Josephine stepped back when John grabbed the horn and pulled himself up onto the horse. The horse bucked wildly.

"Hold on!" she yelled to her husband.

John did his best to do so while the horse turned and twisted and leaped in the air. Josephine ducked between the fence rails and took a perch on the top one.

John held on until…

WHOMP!

He hit the dirt. Josephine covered her mouth to stifle another laugh. John looked at her while the horse pranced around the ring. He picked himself up and brushed the dirt from his pants.

"Be gentle with her, you say," he said to Josephine.

46

The horse came close to John and pawed the dirt. She allowed John to place his hand above her nostrils. Josephine joined them and helped to knock the dust off John's back.

"It was a good effort," she said. "I think she is taking a liking to you."

John responded with a smile, and they kissed.

"I'll let you put her up," John said.

He headed to the barn and Josephine took the reins of the horse.

"I know you're such a good girl," she said to the horse in French while she rubbed the mare's jaw line. "And he is only a man. But you mustn't hurt him. Not this one."

"Josephine, come give me a hand," John yelled from the barn.

Josephine smiled at the horse and walked to the barn. When she entered, John grabbed her. Josephine screamed playfully, for if any man put his hands on her, she certainly wouldn't be the one to scream. He removed her blouse and exposed her breasts. John moved his hand gently along a series of scars that stretched down her back. They kissed deeply and he felt her while she removed his dirty, sweat-stained shirt.

They were interrupted by the sound of a rider approaching. John looked toward the sound, then back at Josephine.

"Ignore it, my love," she said. And he did just that, tasting her nipples.

When the sound of the rider stopped, they knew instinctively that it was a messenger of duty. John released his hold on her.

"Don't stop," she said.

"You think I want to?" he answered. He stroked her hair and helped her to her feet. She put on her blouse and he his shirt.

John came out to greet the rider, replacing the last button on his shirt. The messenger was young but not naive. He turned away and looked toward the cottage while he waited for John. When John was but a few steps away, the soldier turned back and saluted.

"Major Singleton?" he asked.

John returned the salute. "I hope your aim is better than your timing."

When Josephine exited the barn, the messenger looked down at the ground in embarrassment. He extended his hand with a letter to John.

"From General Winder, sir."

John broke the seal, opened it, and read. He looked at the rider, then back to the letter.

"Where is the General now?" asked John.

"At the Capitol, sir," he answered. John looked back toward Josephine.

"Will that be all, sir?"

"Would you like some tea?" asked Josephine.

"No thank you, ma'am," the rider answered. "My orders are to return as soon as possible with Major Singleton."

Josephine looked at her husband. "You have been here for only three days and already they call you back?" she said.

"Tell them I'm on my way," John said to the messenger.

"Major, my orders--"

"Would you rather deal with her, Private?"

The messenger looked at Josephine and saw the woman warrior, scorned. "I'll tell them you are on your way, sir," he said.

The rider saluted, mounted, and left. John walked toward the house and Josephine followed.

"Regular and militia are being called up immediately," he told Josephine.
48

"And you must leave now?"

"Yes."

Josephine cursed in French.

"The English army appears to be docked and ashore," John said. "Landed sometime yesterday."

The words forced Josephine to pause and recall dark and suppressed memories – actions and events that appeared to have followed her to the new world.

"Where?" she asked.

"Near Baltimore. I'm expected in Washington."

"Don't go," said Josephine. "It will be dangerous."

He looked at her somewhat amused. "That's the point, Josephine. You know I must. And I don't trust that Alexandria is out of harm's way. I want you to get your things packed."

"I'm staying right here," she said defiantly. "If I must put up with your coming and going, I'll do it from my own home."

"We can't take any chances. You'll be safer near my parents – or should I say my parents will be safer near you?"

"They can come here. I'm not leaving our home abandoned for just anyone. Especially the English."

He stopped walking and took both of Josephine's hands in his.

"Sometimes I don't know where you're coming from. Please don't fight me over this," he implored.

"You don't have to tell me about war," she answered. "I am too familiar with it already."

"Then you know what I have to do," he said. "I am obligated to my country and my men."

"Just like that?" she said.

"Just like that," he answered.

"And where do I stand in your line of duties?"

"Oh, Josephine," he said. "Must you be so dramatic?"

John finished buttoning his uniform jacket as Josephine watched.

"I came here for peace, and so far there has been nothing but more war," she said. "It is the same everywhere, without exception. And now I have to fall in love with an American soldier."

He pulled his boots on and then took her in his arms. She held him tightly.

"America *is* different," he said. "But that's what makes us most vulnerable. Nobody will fight our fight for us."

"Then I will go with you," she answered. "I'm better with swords. And a better rider."

John smiled and took her face in his hands. He kissed her.

"Perhaps a better rider," he said. "Quite good at a lot of things though, *oui?*"

She moved to leave but he held on to her, kissing her again and stroking her hair.

"Let me fight this one," he said. He caressed her face. "Courage, love. You know I must go."

"Then go!" she snapped. "Do what you have to do. But I'll not leave my home. And don't think I'll always live my life by the expectations of you and your army."

John was used to her defiant spirit. "My God, you are quite a woman."

50

He took his hat, smiled and left her. She cursed under her breath again in French.

Outside, John prepared his horse for travel. He picked up the hind leg and looked at the shoe, careful not to get his blue vest smudged. He stowed his rifle in a bag attached to the saddle and was careful to tighten it just enough. He adjusted his hat for the perfect fit, swung his sword out of the way, and mounted. He trotted a few steps and then turned the horse to look for Josephine.

She hadn't come out of the house. He paused and smiled. He knew this was hard on her but he was confident in the knowledge of her love. He took the reins and headed toward the dirt road.

From the corral, Josephine's dark mare *neighed* and kicked the dirt. Josephine stood at the window, watching John depart until she could stand it no more. She cursed and ran to the door.

"John!" she hollered.

She ran after him into the road. John halted his horse and turned, jumping down to meet her. The two lovers embraced and kissed.

"Stay low in the field," she whispered. "Their aim is usually high. And don't bunch in the center."

Amused, he shook his head and kissed her again.

Josephine stood in the road and watched as he disappeared down the hill. She returned quickly to the house and closed the door behind her. She picked up a teacup and threw it across the room. Wiping away a tear, she then composed herself.

Her horse called for her again. She managed a smile, opened the door, and went back out.

5 REDCOATS AGAIN

The merchants of Baltimore looked out on the bay and muttered their own curses, wrung their hands and talked in whispers. Would it be better to capitulate or more profitable to fight? Even if every slave and every free man worth hiring was put to work to prepare for a siege of some kind, how could they stand against the army that brought down Napoleon? Now the federals wanted their militia and their slaves? The merchants grumbled to themselves and accepted the cost. Money was money and government, whether English or American, only got in the way. The British flagship was just beyond the Baltimore Harbor, anchored with a flotilla of fighting vessels gathered around it like a mother swan and her cygnets. They were too far away to train cannon on but close enough to cause a general anxiety in the city.

On board the ship, Admiral Sir George Cockburn scanned the harbor through his looking glass. Now in his fifties, this hero of the Napoleonic wars stood with a little more casualness, a little more weight, and a biting humor. He saw a boat here and there but nothing out of the ordinary.

"This is most peculiar," he said. "Where is General Ross?"

A nearby aide left to retrieve the general. The Admiral tossed his looking glass to another aide and walked the deck. He looked over the side at the brackish water below and then at his other ships anchored nearby and awaiting orders. It was a fine day to be on the offensive.

General Robert Ross arrived on deck.

"Aaah, there you are," said Cockburn. "Give me your report, General."

General Robert Ross was a bit younger, still with curly black hair but showing signs of aging from war. He was a soldier's soldier, known for his prudence but also his boldness. His Irish wit and bravery in battle had carried him far, and he was secretly admired by men more well known, including Admiral Cockburn.

"Our scouts see no sign of a defense," Ross answered. "Most of our spies believe they know we are here, yet business as usual continues in Washington. I just don't trust it."

"At least Baltimore is offering us a welcoming committee," said Cockburn.

"It would be suicidal to meet us here," answered Ross. "We have the advantage on land and sea. Still, we will have to fight our way through the marines into Baltimore."

"Aah, Barney's marines," answered Cockburn. "You can always count on them. Slippery bastards. I would so love to pick a fight with the Commodore. I owe him one, you know."

"I'm sure you'll have your chance, Admiral," said Ross. "I've not known the Commodore to be reluctant – or any of the Americans, for that matter."

"We shall see, General," said Admiral Cockburn.

"Look here," said Ross, pointing toward a location on a hilltop forest. Cockburn motioned to the midshipman for his spyglass. Through the glass, the Admiral saw a small group of soldiers, maybe marines, and someone looking back at him through his own spyglass. Cockburn smiled.

"So, the game is afoot," said the Admiral. "With our presence known, I imagine their newspapers will be upon us soon. The abuse will work up their readers, sling insults, and worse. Very well, we'd better get a move on."

"This will not be an easy task," said General Ross. "From here, she looks tame. But the Americans are a sleeping tiger."

"Surely, you jest, General," said Cockburn. "Imagine if we had allowed Napoleon this close to Parliament. We'd have two enemies then. Napoleon in front of us, the rabble behind us with their pitchforks and curtain rods, ready to throw us out! I would wager that little James Madison has underestimated our intentions and the people will be ready to cut *his* throat, not ours. May I suggest you take your men ashore to another location?" said Cockburn. "Test the waters before we take Baltimore?"

Ross thought for a moment before offering his reply. His field of play was the land and he and his men were anxious to get there.

"There is much more to gain here in Baltimore," answered Ross. "My men will want to see some action and Parliament will want to parade some bounty. But let's do this, Admiral. I'll take my men inland toward Washington. Let them stretch their legs a bit and see what kind of resistance we come across."

"Well done, General," said Cockburn. "We'll deliver you and your men down the coast. If we have the audacity to march toward Washington, our friends in Baltimore will be only too kind to vacate the city for us without so much as a shot."

"I like your image of simplicity, Admiral," said Ross. "But I have never known war to be such. Destiny can certainly be influenced by the inaction of others. But the Americans are not the kind of people to easily capitulate. We should hold fast for Baltimore. Just consider the trip to Washington an exercise for the men."

"However you want to call it, General," said Cockburn. "You have your troops and a detachment of my marines at your disposal. I want to know your progress. You choose your place, I'll deliver you there. If they are foolish enough to let us get this close, then they deserve to give up some liberties."

"Let's go as far as the town of Benedict, Admiral," answered Ross. "That will give us the lay of the land."

"Very well. It'll be your show on foot, General."

Admiral Cockburn turned to his men on deck. "We shall set a new course. General Ross will pay our Yankee friends a visit!"

A loud cheer sounded across the deck. Ross watched without a show of emotion.

When night fell, the English divided their fleet and pressed the advantage of strength and position. While Cockburn stayed near Baltimore, Ross and his men were escorted down the coast and inland toward the capital. The boats snaked their way up an inlet, using the moonlight and maps from local sympathizers as their guide. Reaching a suitable point, boats were lowered and hatches opened. Seasick horses couldn't wait to get on land. General Ross held the reins to his horse and comforted the great beast with a cube of sugar and a pat on the forehead.

"I don't much care for the water, either," he told the horse. "We shall soon be ashore."

The boats were secured on the small strip of beach and the soldiers made their way onto land. They pushed and pulled the horses up muddy embankments until they entered the woods. The English troops fell into columns. Orderly and with purpose, they marched. They did not wait and did not complain. Most were tired of the ocean and ready for a land fight and the spoils of war.

By the time the sun rose, the army was inland. The steel of their guns reflected in the rays breaking through the trees; the crisp red and white of their uniforms shone bright. A halt was called and General Ross consulted his maps and conferred with his assistants. The soldiers rested on the ground, ate their hardtack, relieved themselves behind trees, and waited for the march to continue.

General Ross rode out of the woods and up a hill, followed by two assistants on horseback. He reached a crest and stopped. From this perspective, all seemed quiet except for the animals and croppers going about their business. The General observed the woods where his men rested and the open fields and roads in front of him. He searched for a trap. For something out of the ordinary. He disbelieved his good fortune on getting the men this far with nary a peep from the Americans, but he knew it wouldn't last. He knew they were being watched. He would not underestimate the Americans nor inflate his own abilities. This was not a time to be reckless.

Secretary Monroe and his aide lay down between the trees and observed General Ross on the far side of the woods. Through his spyglass, Monroe watched the English General. He viewed the forces at rest and the distant bay behind the General to determine their rate of progress and the extent of what they were facing.

"Right, right," Monroe said to himself. "They have moved away from their ships and supplies."

"Not good, sir," said the aide.

"But not bad," Monroe replied. "The General is smelling for a trap, which we have not had the intelligence to set. I'd say he probably has a thousand troops in those woods. Serious business. They don't expect to go back empty handed. By God, if only that jackass Armstrong were here to see this. I'd roll him down this hill right now as a token of peace."

"Sir?"

"Nothing. We'd better get back."

They crawled backward and rode away in a hurry.

Back in Washington, the streets were busy in the capital as words flew with their own wings through every door and every window about an invading English force. People with wagons, horses, whole families, and belongings fought for space on the road. All were leaving the city as quickly as they could, with as much as they could carry.

President Madison looked out at the scene below with a sense of shame. He smoked his pipe to calm his nerves and study the situation. The First Lady joined him.

"What a dreadful sight," she said.

"Word has already sent the city packing," said the President. "They have not even fired a shot, yet the people panic. Panic leads to disorder. Armstrong is right in that regard. Perhaps the English would content themselves with that."

"Hold fast, darling," she said. "We Americans are a stubborn force."

"Damn that Armstrong," replied the President. "He has been a thorn in my side during this whole affair. Now we're exposed. I should have reacted sooner. We have to have the militia here or--"

"Have some brandy, dear. Collect your thoughts. There is nothing a President can do for his country if he doesn't rest."

She poured him a small glass and he took the drink gratefully.

"I'll ride out in a few hours," he said. "Assess the situation myself."

He turned to his wife. "You must be prepared to leave."

She looked at him, not wanting to believe.

"I cannot trust our forces will hold. Damn, imagine what history will think of me."

He put the drink on a table and looked out the window again.

"Damn."

"Dear," she said. "James. Calm yourself. We have been through worse."

"Those were different times," the President answered. "Different people. General Washington would think me a fool now."

"No, darling. War is war. We are in the right. And the right shall always win. No matter what."

Madison smiled at her. "That is what I have always loved about you," he said tenderly. "Life is a romance, always in blossom. We may be in the right, but we are certainly in the way."

She hugged him tightly. He watched as the crowd continued to desert the city.

"I'll wait for your return," she said. "I'll not leave before then."

6 NIGHT

Night had fallen along the country road but one wouldn't know it. Inhabitants filled the road on their way out of the city, forcing John and his horse to the side.

He reached a small cottage that had become the headquarters of the American field command. He dismounted and gave the reins to a soldier on guard.

John entered the cottage and found General Winder bent over the map with his officers. He looked tired and apprehensive at the news he was getting. John saluted and Winder motioned him to the table.

"Major Singleton," said Winder, "I hope this means my militia are here?"

"I have forwarded your requests, sir," answered John. "I'll expect the first lot in the morning."

"Morning," repeated General Winder. "These governors act as if we have all the time in the world. Very well. You'll take your men, when you get them, to the Nottingham-Marlboro road. Hold the bridge at the Tiber. That is your order. If the British come this way, they'll have to cross there."

"If, sir?" said John.

"Best guess, Major. I haven't heard back from our forward parties – or anyone else for that matter."

"There is a strong belief that the aim of the British is Baltimore, sir," John told him. "I'm sure that is the cause of reluctance to give us men."

"Yes, General Smith in Baltimore shares your concerns. The Governor of Maryland will have to get involved to pry his men away. In the meantime, you get your Virginia men in on the double."

John removed a paper from his vest. "I've made a list of supplies for requisition."

"Go to the armory and get what you can," said the General. "Just about everything is gone. You'll have to make do."

"Pardon, sir," answered John. "These men are going to arrive untrained. Some may not even have a weapon."

General Winder paused and nodded. "Confiscate whatever you must," he said. "Sergeant Hill knows a source or two."

"Do we have artillery, sir?"

General Winder grew exasperated with questions to which he couldn't give a proper answer.

"I'm sorry, Major. This is the Army we've got right now. You'll have to make do."

John saluted and turned to leave. When he stepped out, he paused to consider the revelation of the situation. They are ill-prepared for a confrontation.

"Expects us to bring our pitchforks," said a voice from the dark.

John turned to see his old mentor, Sergeant Angus Hill, hobble out of the dark. Although in his late fifties, he had trained many officers, retired, but still had a thirst for action – and now more opportunity had called.

"I'm ready to speak some treasonous words, Sergeant," said John.

"You have my permission, sir," said Hill.

The two friends shook hands.

"How's the lovely French woman?"

"Madder than a hornet."

"God love her."

"You ready for this?" John asked him.

"Well, I thought I'd seen the last of the Redcoats this close to home," Hill replied. "I'll remember what they look like, and I imagine they still die just like they did."

"Where's the best place to gather supplies?" asked John.

"I'm already ahead of you, Major," said Hill. "I've put a couple of warehouses under guard. People are leaving in droves and the thieves are thicker than molasses. I've let the sons-a-bitches go because we may have to do some confiscating ourselves."

"You might just save this war for us, Sergeant," John smiled and said. "It's damn good to see you."

While John and Hill undertook the devil's work outside the capital, night preparations continued in Baltimore. In this game of cat and mouse, both sides organized for unknown targets in an undeclared war. Under the shadow of Fort McHenry, a messenger entered a room and found General Samuel Smith sitting behind a desk piled high with papers. Big and rugged with a curled gray moustache, Smith was a bull that would not be ridden. He had a better nose for war and was preparing for a battle he wasn't sure he could win. But damned if he wouldn't die trying. He didn't look up.

"What is it?" he snapped.

"Request from General Winder, sir," answered the messenger.

General Smith snatched the note and read it. With his pen he scrawled the letters N-O across it and handed it back to the messenger. He stood up.

"Tell General Winder to keep his troubles in Virginia," he said. "I'm not going through hell here to save his ass there."

When the soldier left to return the message to Winder, John and Sergeant Hill headed out with an attaché of local militia and empty carts under a moonlit sky.

Hill removed some tobacco from his mouth and threw it on the ground. "This war has been foolish from the get-go," he said. "The damn politicians. If only my old mates were alive to see this. We've more land and space than we know what to do with and we're still picking fights."

"They came here, Sergeant," answered John. "I don't know too many places that would remain unprovoked in our situation. We're nowhere beaten yet. We're covering the city. Other forces are moved to the river. General Smith's in Baltimore, regardless of where General Winder wants him. And we're here."

"I like your spirit, Major," said Hill. "My gut tells me we're in for quite a whipping though."

"Make declaration!" declared a voice just up the road.

"It's Major Singleton, soldier!" said John. "Sergeant Hill's with me."

A soldier dressed more like a farm hand came out of the shadows. He carried a long stick instead of a gun. John and Hill looked incredulously at each other.

"Yep, quite a whipping," repeated Sergeant Hill.

The soldier saluted. "My gun's in the shop, sir," he explained. "They didn't have no replacement."

John and Hill exchanged another look, then continued on their search. It was sometime in the wee hours of the morning that they approached a farmhouse and knocked at the door.

"Who the hell would knock at this time of night?" a voice asked from inside.

"It's Major Singleton with the local regiment!" John replied.

No answer.

"Hurry up, now!" yelled Hill.

"Are you English or American?" asked the voice.

"It's the English come to bugger your sorry ass, Maynard!" said Hill, laughing to himself.

A man leathery with age and the hard knocks of life opened the door. He looked at John, then at Hill, and smiled slightly.

"Not many have the stones to call me by my Christian name," said Maynard.

"And here I always thought you were dead," answered Hill.

The two men entered the house and Maynard shut the door behind them.

"Follow me," Maynard said. He grabbed a lantern, blew away the dust, and lit it.

"I come across these fairly, Angus," Maynard said. "So don't go trying to screw me out of 'em for God and country and all that shit."

The men walked into the kitchen and watched Maynard pull back some floorboards. The three lifted the box out together, and Maynard opened it with a key. Inside were long rifles – unblemished. John took one, held it in his hands, and checked the sighting.

"They came out of Yorktown," Maynard explained. "The war ended before they were needed and the English left them."

"And you happened to find them," replied Hill with a hint of disbelief.

John checked the sharpness of the bayonet.

"The English know how to make a good rifle," added Maynard. "These may be old but they ain't never been shot. They'll still take a man down if need be."

"How many do you have to sell?" asked John.

"How many do you need?" Maynard answered, raising an eyebrow.

7 MORNING

A night of moving men and weapons from one location to another exhausted the Americans. When the first rays of the sun shed light on his face, John rose and watched the smoke from the untended fires across the American camp. He stretched the stiffness in his bones, splashed water on his face, and put on his field jacket. He kicked Sergeant Hill's boot and the old soldier rose quickly.

"Someone's brewing coffee," said John.

"God bless 'em," said Hill.

"How many came in overnight?" asked John.

"About 300 reported," answered Hill, wiping the sleep from his eyes.

"That's well short of our needs," said John.

"I interspersed them with the regulars, but I'll be truthful, most of 'em would do better scaring crows from a cornfield."

They walked a ways surveying the camp and stopped near a pot of coffee. A man handed cups of the steaming liquid to both of them. Sgt. Hill removed a small bottle from inside his vest and emptied it into the cup.

"There's a lot of rumors going around," said Hill. "What occurred with the regulars in Detroit. Up in Newark. Got 'em plum scared the British are coming to retaliate. I'm a wee bit concerned we'll have some runners when the fighting starts."

"Aah, well," surmised John. "The day is ripe for discussion on how quickly we go to our deaths, it seems. Let's gather the men."

"Aye, sir."

Hill grabbed an old metal pan and beat on it with a stick.

"Attention!! Attention!! Rise and shine on the double!! Prepare for address!!"

The men left their tents or picked themselves up from around the morning fires and gathered near Hill and John. Some were quick, some were less so. Some filled their mouth with the last morsel of food and sip of coffee they could. Others tied up suspenders, urinated, or struggled to pull on muddy sun-baked boots.

"Form your lines! Form your lines!" shouted Hill.

Men meandered about, lost and needing direction.

"You want the taste of British steel in your arse?" yelled Hill. He stuck a boot into the back end of a soldier who then moved quickly to join a line.

"How far we've fallen," Hill muttered to himself.

Most of these men were not professional soldiers and not familiar with military décor. The men picked up the pace and finally fell into line. Some were kids, others were grandfathers. Most were dirty and right off the farm. Their skill at shooting squirrels and deer was as close to shooting men that they had come. Sergeant Hill removed his cap and looked toward the ground.

"Say what you want to say," said John.

"We would do best to pull back and wait for the regulars," said Hill.

"I have doubts of seeing any enlisted men outside of Baltimore," said John. "Besides, our ability to offer any delay fully depends on the initiative of the British."

John moved away from Hill to find a more advantageous spot to address his men.

"Attention!" Hill yelled.

66

The men stood straighter and observed John.

"Good morning, men!" yelled John. "My name is Major John Singleton. It is my privilege to lead you in the defense of our country. Now I know many of you have not fought in battle before. Neither had our fathers when the Redcoats came the first time. Yet here we are again, defending our families and our freedom!

John paused to let his words hang in the air. He surveyed his men from one end of the line to the other.

"The British are here to take anything you own away from you! And anything else they can get their hands on. They mean to reclaim what they believe is theirs!"

"When they came the first time, they said we wouldn't last," continued John. "They were wrong then, and they will be wrong now. We are still here. We're not going anywhere. We threw them off this land once and by God, we're going to throw them all off again!"

A loud shout of approval erupted from the men, and they were ordered at ease by Sergeant Hill.

"Go ahead and distribute what we have, Sergeant," said John.

"Aye, Major."

Sergeant Hill whistled and a soldier hauled a horse and wagon up to them. John and Hill threw back the canvas to reveal a pile of collected rifles. Some were shiny and new; others in various stages of heavy use.

"Step up and get a weapon if you need one," Hill ordered. He pulled rifles from the wagon and handed them to the soldiers. One lanky young man approached John.

"Excuse me, sir?"

"Yes?"

"Do you have any shoes, sir?"

John looked down at the man's bare feet.

"My God, man, how did you get here?"

"I walked, sir. I've got my own gun, but I could sure use a pair of shoes."

"Sergeant Hill?"

"Yes, sir?"

"Have we found any shoes?"

"I'll see what I can find, sir."

"See to it, Sergeant."

"Yes, sir."

John directed his attention back to the soldier.

"Get one of the empty potato sacks for now and cut them into strips."

"Yes, sir," replied the soldier.

John motioned for Sergeant Hill to leave the wagon to others and join him.

"Add shoes to the list of confiscation, Major?" asked Hill.

"Yes, Sergeant," answered John. "What kind of cannon do we have?"

"Two eight pounders," answered Hill. "All I could get. Most are with General Smith."

"I wonder what General Winder thinks we're going to accomplish here with only one pair of boomers?"

"Like you said, Major," answered Hill. "We're going to give him time. And if that's not enough, we're going to give some blood as well."

They finished dispersing the rifles and walked around the camp, inspecting the line of defense and preparing for the British assault. John stopped in front of a boy, and the boy saluted.

"How old are you?" asked John.

"Old enough, sir," answered the boy.

John and Hill waited for a more specific answer.

"Thirteen, sir," said the boy, "but I can shoot straight and kill as many Redcoats as you need."

"Where's your rifle?" asked John.

"My pa wouldn't let me bring it," answered the boy. "He's laid up with a bad back so he sent me. We only have one rifle so he needed to keep it. On account of my ma and my little brothers and sisters. He says if you want me the least you can do is supply the rifle."

John approved of the boys courage. He took a rifle from a soldier carrying two and gave it to the boy. It was heavy and nearly as big as him, but the boy tried to hold back his excitement.

"Stay low," said John. "They usually aim high."

"Yes, sir!" said the boy.

They continued their walk among the men and came to an old man with a long beard. He already had his own rifle and saluted the men when they approached.

"I'll get at least two of the bastards before they get me," the old man said proudly.

"I'll expect you to get three, sir," said John.

The old man smiled and showed the only two teeth in his head. He saluted again and John and Hill continued on.

"You have any more prizes for us, Sergeant?" asked John. "Any artillery you can think of?"

"I'm still looking, Major," said Hill. "I know another old codger we can ask. Would sell it to the British if it meant more coin to him though."

"Sergeant, set the men at ease and then visit your friend. Visit every house between here and there. Muster a detachment and collect what we need. But be mindful of your surroundings. At this stage, wouldn't surprise me to see more locals give way to their fears and act accordingly."

"Good thinking, sir," answered Hill.

Hill left and John mulled the options in front of him. If not for the preparations at hand and the looming threat of contact with the enemy, the day would be remembered as one of God's best. The sky was clear and blue with the exception of flocks of geese and ducks migrating from one water source to another. While the men labored to become soldiers overnight and establish their lines of defense, the women and children back home, on the farms and the cottages that dotted the coastal lakes and rivers, kept right on working. There was no time to stop for war and no time to waste worrying when crops demanded to be harvested and livestock required attending to.

John's situation was no different than these men. He was a professional soldier yet he also had the responsibility of a farm to run. He smiled when his thoughts turned to Josephine. He had chosen wisely and was secure in knowing that she could handle things when he was called away, that she'd be there on his return, and that one day she would bare him as many children as their farm could support.

For her part, Josephine didn't like being alone on the farm, but it was her home and she threw herself into the work. She learned new skills and adapted rather quickly. She had been trained to be mindful of the task at hand, and to be purposeful and engaged until the deed was done. It translated rather well to the tasks on the farm, where she also learned patience and the joy of the work, not just the result.

Josephine pulled water from the well while the mare roamed freely in the field. She carried the two filled buckets into the house, careful not to spill any, and placed them on the sideboard. She walked to a cabinet to remove a pitcher when suddenly, one of the buckets cracked. The water seeped over the sideboard and onto the floor and found its way through the wooden grooves of the floor. Josephine carried the cracked bucket outside. She returned and dropped down on her hands and knees, using a rag to sop up the water. She looked at the grooves in the floor where the water had run, then sat back on her heels in thought.

She removed several planks of the floor with her hands, revealing her long wooden box with the initials "LL." She put her hands below the floor and wiped away the drops of water from the lid. She opened the lid and touched her uniform. She placed the uniform aside and removed the pistols. Almost without thinking she palmed and then twirled them. She cocked and pointed them at imaginary targets.

Josephine lay them on the uniform and picked up one of the daggers. She twirled it in her hand to feel its weight. To see whether it moved the same. It had been so long. She noticed a spider crawling on the wall. With a flick of her wrist, the dagger flew across the room and...*thwack!* Pinned the spider to the wall.

Then the swords – still sharp, still dangerous. She held them in her hands for the first time in years. She stood and made a cutting motion with them. She was rusty, but it felt good to have them in her hands – it felt right to her.

It felt comforting.

8 ASHORE

Admiral Cockburn sat on the forward deck of his flagship at a small desk brought out for that purpose. He wrote notes in the ship's journal with a half cup of tea and some biscuits nearby. An aide approached.

"What's your report?" Cockburn asked.

"General Ross and his army have encamped near Benedict, sir."

Cockburn put his pen down with a look of surprise.

"No resistance?" he asked.

"A small detachment of Maryland regulars surrendered, sir. General Ross reported no further appearances."

Cockburn leaned back in his chair, surveying the harbor and his fighting flotilla. *It is destiny, isn't it?* he thought to himself.

"You see, I told him!" Cockburn said. "That puts us within striking distance of Washington!"

He paused to consider his next move. "Get a boat ready," he ordered. "And transfer my flag to Brooks. We shall meet General Ross and offer him further encouragement."

Cockburn drank down the tea, rose from his chair, and tugged on his vest to straighten it.

"Destiny calls, gentlemen," said Cockburn. "I shall have to impress upon General Ross the inevitability of all this. I know his mannerism. He will change his mind toward prudence in due course. I'll have to be there when he does."

The aides scurried away and Cockburn began to scheme. If the Americans could be provoked to defend their capital, the less resources Baltimore would have. But would they defend it? The crown still had many friends here. Many loyalists. But first he would have to provoke Ross.

Near Benedict, Ross knelt in a pastureland and observed the wildflowers. He had made good time, much better than expected, and with few signs of hostility. He looked up and proudly watched the procession of soldiers in front of him. Many saluted and called his name. He nary offered a smile but returned every salute with a nod or a salute of his own.

"Good morning, General!" they said. "Good day for battle, sir!" "Beautiful morning!"

"That it is, men!" he answered them.

He would die for these men, and they for him. They were professionals and had been in battles across Europe together. Though they were crossing through a foreign land, many felt the American states to be a piece of themselves. Perhaps a long lost brother, or the prodigal son. An unfinished business to which they had returned.

General Ross picked a flower and held it gently in his hands. He felt the texture of the petals and it reminded him of silk as he rubbed it. He noticed a church atop a nearby hill, surrounded by the buggies and horses of the parishioners. Above the movement of his soldiers, he could hear *singing* coming from inside the church. It was a tune he knew and he began humming it to himself. He tossed the flower to the ground and strode toward the church. His aides fell in behind him and tried to catch up.

Inside the church, the minister led the hymn with vigor and hand motions. Some of his flock were already eyeing the scene outside the windows, and he gazed out the window with them. From their point of view, they could see General Ross as he approached the church on foot with some of his men behind him. The song caught in the minister's throat and the singing sputtered to a stop.

Children ran to the windows to gawk. Some of the adults gasped and whispered in fear.

"Let's stay calm now," offered the minister.

The churchgoers emptied their pews to further watch the scene and soon made their way outside. General Ross approached and recognized the apprehension on the faces of the people.

"Corporal!" the General called behind him.

"Yes, sir."

"Go back and ensure the men take rest," said Ross.

"Is it wise--"

"I shan't be long."

"Yes, sir," answered the Corporal, and he motioned the soldiers to return with him, leaving Ross alone.

Ross removed his hat as he approached. The minister came from behind his flock and stood in front of them.

"Everyone stay still," said the minister. "Stay calm. This is holy ground, and no place for fear."

Ross bowed deeply with his hat in hand. The people were bewildered and one man with only one arm reached for his concealed gun. The pastor noticed and motioned for him to stop.

"I beg your apologies for this disturbance," said General Ross. "My men won't be long at rest before we continue. I was so enjoying your hymns that I had wished to hear them closer."

"There is only peace here, sir," said the minister. "What are your intentions?"

"Minister, You and your people have nothing to fear from us. Our grievances rest with your government."

"We are the government!" exclaimed a church member.

When Ross looked at the man, his demeanor changed visibly.

"Perhaps you should go inside and pray then, sir," he said. "Pray for your government and for the mercy not shown my comrades over several years of hostilities. Pray hard. Because judgment day is coming."

General Ross put on his hat, tipped it to the minister, and walked away. The one-armed man reached for his gun again. The minister had to forcibly stop him.

"Christians!" said the minister. "I heard a good suggestion! Let us go in and continue the service. And let us pray."

Whilst the English continued their march, John and Hill worked miracles to prepare the American forces. Many of their men lolled near the bridge and the road, tending to fires, sharing stories, while waiting for arms and ammunition to arrive. John saluted a messenger and had just sent him off to General Winder when they heard the sound of more riders approaching.

"Aaww, it's Jemmy," said Hill.

"You know Secretary Monroe?" asked John.

"We've shared a hole or two."

Secretary Monroe and his aide reined their horses to a halt. The Secretary looked more like a military man now, a pistol at his side and a rifle in his saddlebags.

John approached and saluted.

"Mr. Secretary," said John. "It's Major Singleton."

"Of course, Major," replied Monroe with a salute.

"And you know Sergeant Hill?" added John.

"Angus," Monroe greeted Hill.

"Jemmy, how are ya'?" asked Hill.

"A fine situation we're in if it's up to our old bones to get us out of this," answered Monroe with a smile.

"You politicians have really done it this time," replied Hill.

"Their force is ashore at the Patuxent," Monroe said to them. "They've slowed a bit either out of caution or for reinforcements."

"You're sure, sir?" asked John.

"I saw them myself," answered Monroe. "We are too tempting a target with our lack of preparation. I must apologize to you, Major. You will bear the brunt of our government's neglect. Any scorn the future has for men of my position will be well deserved."

"We'll hold them, sir," John told him, "but I don't need to tell you the urgency with which we need reinforcements."

Monroe looked around at the American army assembled.

"God help us," he said. "We've squandered most of our forces elsewhere. I'm on the way back for another look-see at the enemy. Why don't you join me, Major? I owe you the opportunity to make your own impression."

"Go ahead, sir," added Hill. "We'll keep busy right here."

John walked away to retrieve his horse.

"You didn't ask me to come," said Hill.

"The battle will come soon enough, Angus," said Monroe. "You'll be cursing me then so it's better that we maintain some distance."

"Aah hell, Jemmy," said Hill, "wasn't like I had anything better to do. I owes you one anyway."

Secretary Monroe led his aide and John toward the location of the enemy. Meanwhile, meeting no enemy of their own and suffering no impunities, General Ross kept his men moving farther into the countryside – farther than anyone would have imagined. Ross had used the stop near the church to map his possible routes and to place men at intervals behind him should a hasty retreat be necessary. But no real obstacle presented itself and the bulk of his army made good time and offered no complaint for rest. They would've marched all the way to Washington in anticipation of glory was it not for Ross, who finally stopped them in a picturesque area near a rolling stream, cornfield, and a thick patch of woods.

General Ross dismounted and took up residence at the foot of an old patriarch oak. He checked his map and then glanced at his pocket watch. He was in a fairly good frame of mind until he saw Admiral Cockburn approaching on horseback with his aides. Ross stood up and dusted himself off.

"I did not expect you, Admiral," said Ross in greeting.

"I must say I'm impressed with your expediency, General," Cockburn replied.

"The weather is fair and the road is unrestricted thus far," explained Ross.

Ross took his hat off and surveyed the pastoral scene around him and the giant shade tree under which he stood. "It is really a fine province," said Ross.

"A few too many pints and I would swear I was on some back road in Yorkshire," agreed Cockburn.

Ross replaced his hat. "We should be coming up on a hamlet called Nottingham," Ross said. "We'll make camp there, then proceed toward Benedict. Do you plan to join us or return to your ships?"

"It was right kind of our Yankee brothers and sisters to carry the names of old England here," replied Cockburn. "Makes one feel right at home. I think I'll stay awhile, General, and see what mischief we can cause."

An English soldier approached the general and the admiral.

"General Ross, we found someone," he said.

A pair of soldiers brought forward an old man – dirty, disheveled, and with few teeth.

"We caught him spying on us from the trees, sir."

"That's a bunch of beeswax!" cried the old man. "I was walking my own proper-tay. You red-bellied bastards are trespassing! And if you continue down this road, you're going to get your king-loving arses kicked all the way back to England!"

The soldiers couldn't help but express amusement at the old man's defiance. General Ross broke his own first smile.

"I beg your pardon for the intrusion, sir," said General Ross. "We shan't be here long and will leave your property."

"Your men took my pig," the old man said accusingly. "My sow!"

Ross looked at the two men restraining him.

"Is this true?" he asked.

"We don't know, sir," answered one of the soldiers sheepishly. Ross looked hard at him.

"It's possible, sir," acquiesced the soldier.

General Ross reached into his chest pocket and pulled out a few bank notes. "Will you accept British pounds for your trouble?" Ross asked the old man.

The old man looked at his captors and figured he had little option. "They'll spend," he muttered.

General Ross put some notes in the old man's extended hand.

"If you would allow my men to escort you back to your home, I'm sure we can accommodate you and avoid any further unpleasantries."

"Don't try that high-talking English shit on me," replied the old man angrily. "Tell your men to stay away from the rest of my livestock!"

"Have you seen any American soldiers, sir?" Cockburn interrupted.

"I ain't seen nothing!" exclaimed the old man. "But we kicked your arses once, and we'll do it again if we has to!"

Cockburn leaned back and smiled at the defiant boldness of the old man.

"Sir, we are now only a few miles from your capitol," Cockburn explained. "Where in God's name are your soldiers?"

The old man smiled wickedly. "They's planning a welcoming party for ya'."

"Escort this man back to his home," said Ross abruptly. The General tipped his hat to the old man. "Until we meet again," Ross said.

As they led the old man away, he hollered over his shoulder. "And you can tell Wellington and the King to kiss my *arse*, too!"

Admiral Cockburn motioned to another soldier to come forward.

"Yes, sir?"

"Give that man a good knock on the head if he slings any further insults against the King."

"Yes, sir."

"Any further reports from our scouting parties?" the Admiral asked General Ross.

"They have not yet returned," answered Ross. "Nevertheless, we have come much farther inland than I believed the Americans would allow. It is damn peculiar."

"It is sloth," answered Cockburn. "They have grown fat and foolish off this land."

Just then, a shot rang out from an unknown source. The soldiers nearby brought their weapons to the ready and looked toward the source. Cockburn leaned closer to his horse and searched the woods. General Ross didn't move but scanned the horizon with his spyglass. From his point of view, nothing had changed; the farm, the cornfield, the stream, the woods – nothing more – not a puff of smoke or a glint of metal.

Another shot hit a supply wagon and spooked Cockburn's horse, nearly throwing the Admiral. This time, Ross sighted smoke rising from the distant woods.

"There you are," he said to himself.

In the woods, Secretary Monroe watched through his spyglass while his aide and John reloaded their rifles. Monroe saw the British soldiers searching for someone to shoot, and watched as General Ross stood defiantly and Admiral Cockburn brought his horse under control.

"That must be General Ross," said the Secretary. "I have heard of him. All good until he landed here. Brave red-belly, I'll give him that. And there's that bastard, Cockburn. Him I know. If he has come ashore, away from his ships, that can mean only trouble."

Secretary Monroe tossed his spyglass to his aide and took the rifle. John hugged his rifle to his cheek and took aim.

"Maybe we could end this right here with a good shot," said John.

"Yes, Major," answered Monroe. "Damn. I'd give one of them a plug right now if I wasn't such a gentleman. Hope I don't regret it."

"I'll be glad to do it for you, sir," said John.

"The rules of war, Major. The damned rules of war."

John lowered his rifle and took up the spyglass himself. "They're moving artillery. A dragoon. Two regiments."

John saw a line of five soldiers as they prepared to fire toward the woods. "Brace yourselves," he warned.

The volley of fire pierced the trees, spraying splinters of wood all around them.

"Let's give them one more greeting and then be on our way," said Monroe.

John and Secretary Monroe returned the fired, forcing more of the British soldiers to take up positions.

"Oh, how I miss the action!" said the Secretary. He resembled a happy English gentleman on a fox hunt, eagerly reloading the rifle himself this time.

"Time to move, sir," said the aide.

Monroe was caught up remembering the days he and Angus Hill fought for General Washington.

"What a sensation," the Secretary said. He set his rifle against the tree to shoot again.

"Mr. Secretary," John said, "I think we've accomplished what we came for."

"Oh, alright," answered the Secretary.

He lowered his rifle and they backed away through the woods, mounted their horses, and quickly galloped off. After some time, they came to an unmarked crossroads and stopped.

"This is where I take my leave, Major," said the Secretary.

"We'll be ready," John replied. "We'll hold until reinforcements arrive."

"You'll have to hold them," said the Secretary. "Truth is, I don't know if the President is still in Washington. I need you to carry our findings to General Winder and I'll do everything I can to get General Smith to release his men from Baltimore."

"If we could at least get more rifles and artillery," John implored.

"On my order, you requisition what you need from who you need," said the Secretary. "Even at gunpoint. If that jackass Armstrong had been ready, we wouldn't be in this situation."

They saluted one other.

"Good luck, Major," said the Secretary, and he departed with his aide.

We'll need more than luck, John thought to himself.

9 FAIR WEATHER

When night approached, a driving rain accompanied by a series of thunderbolts turned the once-pristine landscape into mud. The British encampment was a sea of wet tents flapping against the wind. Lanterns and fires fought to stay lit as horses pulled nervously against their posts.

General Ross adjusted the lantern in his tent and sat down on his cot with his legs folded. He absentmindedly spooned food from a bowl to his mouth as he looked out the opening of the tent. Lightning revealed the empty camp, with the storm driving the men inside their tents for shelter.

Ross put his bowl aside, picked up a journal, and jotted a few notes in it. When lightning struck again, he looked out. This time he was surprised to see what appeared to be a woman and a boy standing under a tree in the distance. More thunder and the darkness returned. At the next lightning strike, the image was gone.

Ross wondered at what he saw, and his mind tried to dismiss the belief in omens that were prevalent among the warrior class. He looked back at Cockburn, who was lying on his own cot and picking his teeth in front of a hand mirror.

"Yes, General?" said Cockburn. "What's on your mind?"

Ross decided to say nothing about the apparition and resumed eating.

"I'm surprised we haven't seen more negroes," said Cockburn. "What an opportunity they have with our presence here. Once we strike, they will run from their plantations and their masters like ants to a picnic."

Cockburn threw his toothpick away and looked at his teeth in the hand mirror.

"The land of democracy," Cockburn continued. "Rubbish. This place is full of hypocrites. The Americans are nothing more than renegade Britons. We will set our brothers straight."

"We are the invaders, Admiral," Ross reminded him.

"We are the liberators, General," Cockburn countered. "These American politicians are interested in freedoms so long as someone else pays for it. They have no problem removing the liberties of another. Greed is what built this country. And greed is what will undo it."

He lowered the mirror and turned to the General.

"You have too much Irish in you, Ross. That little man Madison in the palace up there? He doesn't care about democracy or liberty. He cares about position! What is the purpose of this country but to extract resources for the rich and restrain the weary? History will remember us as liberators, I tell you."

"Pardon me, Admiral," answered Ross. "Your talk is noble, but I must remind you that in many respects, this war is unnecessary. We have France in tatters. Our enemies are at bay. There is nothing to fear from the Americans. And our mission was to remain in Baltimore without further provocation or retribution."

"Yes, you are right, General, as usual," Cockburn replied. "But if we are to maintain the rule of law in Europe and replenish the treasury, it will take more than what Baltimore has to offer. This land was once the King's property. Paid for and bought by our ancestors. A few of your own as well, General."

Cockburn moved closer to Ross. "Think of it. We can strike a blow that will cripple the memory of this insurrection. First, Washington. Then back to Baltimore. We have come this far with very little resistance. I tell you, they are unprepared. We can sweep away--"

"Our orders are Baltimore, sir, with good reason," Ross interrupted. "We can liberate enough bounty there that I'm sure will help the cause at home and stop their lust for Canada – not to mention the good it will do for our own reputations. We are moving ourselves too far from supplies with this expanded objective."

Cockburn held his tongue as Ross rose from his cot and paused to take in the wet night sky.

"Still, I must admit, Admiral, I have thought more about your suggestions. If we were not so far from your ships, I would be tempted to pursue the opportunity you speak of."

Cockburn smiled confidently and walked to his side.

"Put your mind at rest, General," he said. "I took the liberty of ordering the flotilla farther inland before I came to join you. Our marines and sailors should be moving up from Pig's Point as we speak."

Ross looked at Cockburn with a mixture of surprise and respect for his cleverness.

"Washington has been your goal all along," said Ross.

"Listen to reason, General. You said it yourself. We are the keepers of our own destiny. And our destiny is to take Washington and recover this country. We must take Washington and liberate it from these rebels!"

"I left a hundred men at Marlborough to guard our rear," answered Ross. "That is not enough should we be forced to retreat."

"Aah! You are over-estimating their attention and abilities!"

"And you are over-estimating ours!"

Cockburn sensed that he had pushed Ross far enough and moved back to his cot.

"Alright, General, alright," he said. "I have always known you to be a man of prudence and sensible courage. Let us sleep on it. Often times, a good night's sleep clears the mind for the present."

Cockburn swung his long legs up onto the cot.

"I will not break away from the orders given unless you are with me," said Cockburn. "If you are still disinclined in the morning, I will abide by your decision."

He rolled over and pretended to rest. He calculated the success of the conversation and the play for Ross's consent, smiling to himself. Ross looked away from the Admiral. The storm had died down, and a full moon peaked out from behind clouds.

From another vantage point near the capital, the same full moon peered down over a long line of American men, boys, and regular soldiers moving among a field of campfires. The storm had bypassed their encampment and each soldier waited in the dark for a bowl of mush ladled up with a hunk of bread and one small dried fish.

Inside the makeshift headquarters, General Winder conferred with his staff over a map. John and Sergeant Hill looked wet and tired from their ride into the camp, and they shook the rain from their clothes at the door.

John and Hill saluted in unison and Winder returned the salute.

"The British are a day's march away," said John. "Cavalry, foot soldiers, a full regiment. Secretary Monroe pointed out a General Ross and Admiral Cockburn."

The men quietly looked at one another as the news sunk in.

"Then the rumors are true," General Winder said, breaking the silence. "Scrap the previous orders. Major Singleton, you'll take the regiment here back to Bladensburg with you. The British will have to cross there if they intend to reach Washington. Establish a picket as close as you can. I don't want any forces converging on that bridge until our other units arrive."

"Sir, if we send a forward unit, we might dissuade them," John suggested. "Buy us some more time."

"We are not even at half strength as it is," answered the General. "I'll not risk casualties until reinforcements arrive. Besides, I must confer with the President. You men have your orders. And Major Singleton, you'll accompany me."

"Sir, I have much preparation to attend to," said John.

"Let Sergeant Hill do it," answered Winder. "I need the President to hear about this from more than just me."

Winder turned and left, followed by John, who stopped by Hill on his way out.

"You are quite popular," said Hill.

"He's afraid of delivering the news himself," answered John. "You know what to do, Sergeant?"

"That I do, sir."

General Winder, his aides, and John left the field command and galloped toward the White House. Another regiment of soldiers was spread across the grounds in their tents, preparing for a siege of the city. The riders were stopped and then escorted to the President.

Two soldiers stood at guard while the President reviewed his own map with Monroe and Armstrong. When the guards saluted, Madison turned to see who was entering. Monroe and John acknowledged one another.

"General Winder," said the President. "Just in time. Secretary Monroe has brought me up to speed. What is our strength now?"

"We have about two thousand men between here and the location of the enemy," the General answered.

"Damn!" interjected the President. "It is not enough."

"Philadelphia and New York have answered the call," continued Winder. "They should be arriving with Barney's marines. Baltimore has so far denied the request and is preparing a defense of their own. We've done our best in the time given."

"We are light on both men and weaponry, General," explained the President. "And now it seems from what Secretary Monroe is telling me, we are certainly the target. And still, General Smith will not come to our aid. I'm not sure if I blame him. So, what is your strategy, General Winder?"

The General hesitated before answering. "I've already stationed forces forward under the command of Major Singleton, but if we don't get relief from Barney or from Baltimore, then we fight and we pray. And if that doesn't work, Mr. President, we might better seek terms."

The men exchanged a look of alarm at Winder's suggestion.

"This is poppycock!" blasted Armstrong. "They are too far from their supplies and their ships!"

General Winder scrunched his hat with white knuckles. "Mr. Secretary, If you had approved my requests weeks ago--"

"Enough!" interrupted the President.

"They are coming," Secretary Monroe spoke up. "We must be prepared to evacuate the capital – gain time and consolidate our men."

"The armory is still open!" exclaimed Secretary Armstrong.

"The armory has been empty for some time!" General Winder replied angrily. "My men come back empty-handed. We find more on the open market than we do in our own warehouses!"

"Where are your forces now, Major?" asked the President.

John went to the map and the men circled around it. Pointing, he said, "General Winder's men are here and will be regrouped with my men here at Bladensburg crossing on the north side of the bridge."

"I need a realistic assessment of the outcome," said the President.

President Madison looked at each man and stopped when he came back to John. "You're in the belly of the beast, Major," said the President. "I need a frank assessment of our chances."

Monroe urged John on with a nod of his head.

"The men I have charge of are willing but not ready. Most came straight from their fields and not all of them are armed. If we can hold out long enough for Commodore Barney's men or General Smith and some of the regulars to arrive, that is the best we can hope for. And if they advance an attack before then?"

The assembled men waited for John to answer his own question. "Maybe we can hold for a day and a night," he finished.

General Winder, ashamed, changed his tune. "We'll fight, Mr. President! God help us, we'll fight."

"We have no choice but to fight, General," said the President. "And should the British carry the day--"

Madison stopped himself mid-sentence and reconsidered his statement. "We shall remove ourselves from the capital and continue the fight another day. Our goal of these next few days is to not let the war end here. No matter the loss."

The President turned to Major Singleton. "I'll ride out to see the men before I leave."

"Yes, sir," answered John.

The President left the tent. Armstrong moved to join him but Winder grabbed him by the arm.

"How dare you!" sneered Armstrong, pulling away.

"God help me, history will know of your role in this," General Winder said, glaring at Armstrong.

Without a word, Armstrong left the tent to catch up with the President.

"I hate that man," Winder growled.

Monroe hesitated, wanting to add his own thought. Thinking better of it, he looked at John and then left.

"I'll return to my men, sir," John said to Winder, who nodded. Knowing what John was up against, he offered his hand instead of a salute.

"Sorry for putting you in this situation, Major," said Winder. The men shook hands and John revealed no emotion about the daunting task facing him.

John walked out, leaving Winder alone with the maps and the fear of approaching defeat.

10 THE MARINES

Waves lapped against the docks, boats, and merchant vessels anchored along the Baltimore Harbor. A sizeable presence of American gunships were tied in berths along a wooden dock that protruded a great distance parallel to the shore. With the arrival of Cockburn, the United States navy had been caught off balance and at rest. And now, outsized and outnumbered by the blockade, there was nowhere to go. Under cover of darkness, a group of American marines raced down the dock, running a trail of gunpowder from the warships back to a safe distance on land.

Commodore Barney looked grim, more grim than usual for the wind-whipped sailor who had cut his teeth on the open seas. The creases in his face were like a roadmap of the new nation. He spit a chaw of tobacco on the ground and prepared to do what had to be done.

"Take the flag down, goddammit," Barney barked. "You forgot the flag, idiot!"

"Are you sure about this, sir?" asked a marine.

"I'd rather blow them all to hell than let the cocksuckers have 'em," Barney growled. "And I'm not gonna let the flag burn!"

The last of the powder was emptied from the key and snaked away from the fleet. The marines grouped together with Barney behind a pile of rocks. They waited for Barney to say the word but he spit out tobacco juice instead.

"We're ready, sir," said a marine.

"Then do it," Barney said gruffly.

A marine put a spark to the powder. It ignited and raced for the ships.

"Cover your arses!" yelled Barney.

The flame showered sparks as it snaked toward the flotilla. But then it suddenly went out.

"Aw, hell!" yelled Barney.

He clambered out from behind the rocks.

"Sir!" shouted a marine.

"Shut up!" said Barney. "Jee-sus, no wonder they came. Have to do the damn thing myself."

Barney left abruptly to do a young man's job. He removed flint from his pocket and set a spark to the powder. It reignited and he ran for safety. His men grabbed him and pulled him behind the rock.

"How many kegs did you use?" Barney asked.

"Twenty, sir."

"Jee-sus."

The men looked at the flotilla of boats that comprised most of the American navy. Schooners, skimmers, and barges were now set to take their final mission.

KA-BOOM!! BOOM!! BOOM!! BOOM!!

The exploding ships shook the entire vicinity awake.

In their encampment, Ross and Cockburn awoke from the explosions and stared at each other.

John reined in his horse and looked toward the sound.

Josephine sat in a corner of her darkened home in a defensive position hugging her knees with her eyes peering over the tops of them. Moonlight streamed through the window when she heard the *explosion* in the distance.

Her horse *neighed* for her and she recited her mantra. It took all of her energy to keep from springing into action, from doing something deadly. The waiting – the knowledge of a threat and that John was out there somewhere and she was just sitting there – was not part of her warrior's code. She was in a different place wearing a different kind of mask being the good and faithful wife. It was not something the Master taught her and it was killing her. She recited the mantra, hoping for strength of patience, and she cried in frustration.

Near the capital, a group of American soldiers and slaves armed with axes and shovels worked to block an entryway to the city. Torches lit their objectives and they hacked away, dragged trees, and shoveled dirt in a long line.

"Someone's coming!" called out a sentry.

The soldiers grabbed their rifles. The sentry stepped forward, rifle at the ready. "Identify yourself!" the sentry hollered

"At ease, soldier," said a weary voice in the dark. "It's General Winder."

The soldiers looked at each other in amazement. Winder came in to view, holding his shoulder as he walked toward them. He tossed a small empty bottle from which he'd been drinking. The sentry lowered his rifle, curious at seeing the General on foot.

"My horse threw me," said the General in explanation, trying to catch his breath. "I must've walked three miles. One helluva explosion."

He took a handkerchief out and wiped his brow. "How goes it here?"

"The road is being obstructed as ordered, sir."

"As ordered? Who gave that order?"

"You did, sir."

General Winder looked first at the soldier, then at the work being done, and the other soldiers. He did not recall giving the order and he rubbed his shoulder.

"Yes, I guess I did," he said. "Well, carry on then. And see if you can find me a fresh bottle and a horse. I meant to say a fresh horse. You know what I mean."

John's camp was active and busy in a hurry to prepare. With fires burning for warmth and light, dirt flew from shovels as protective earthen piles were formed up. Men shared meals, water, and booze; others cleaned their weapons, moved cannon, and found the best positions from which to mount the defense.

John walked past the fires and past the diggers. He looked tired as he observed the distant hills under the stars and the flat land between them and where he anticipated the enemy advance. Sergeant Hill joined him and offered a drink of whiskey. John declined.

"If I were them," said John, looking across the way, "I would set position there. Do you agree, Sergeant?"

"Yes, sir," said Hill.

"Then we need to have men on that ridge."

"I'll make it happen, sir."

"Where's the regulars that reported?"

"I split them up, Major"

John looked at him. "I don't think the British should see us this fragmented," he said.

"I understand, sir. I thought it best not to group our regulars. Figured they'd draw all the fire and be gone before the battle even started."

"Maybe you're right," said John.

"Sometimes I can be, sir," answered Hill. "Can I get you some vittles?"

John waved him off and Hill left to continue duties. John climbed toward the ridge to make another observation. When he reached the top, he took off his hat and looked back at his men. It wasn't a polished army but it was the best available. Many were young and would be unprepared for the
94

approaching engagement. Many would die. John ran a hand through his hair. *My God, what have we forced ourselves into?* he thought to himself.

John knew what death was. He had earned his stripes in Ontario, battling the British and the Mohawks until the Americans were routed and his wounds had sent him home. He thought he would die then and he wasn't afraid to die now. Honor and duty were his obligation – more important than life itself. But now there was Josephine. What about Josephine?

John sat down against a tree, and for a few moments, he let his thoughts turn to her. If anyone could take care of herself, it was this French beauty he'd found. He smiled in admiration of her. Their time together had been brief and she was still more of a mystery to him than most wives would be. She was different than any woman he had known – stronger than most men, which he found attractive. He couldn't help but remember the awkwardness of their courtship and he smiled again. He had approached Josephine as most men would, assuming a certain masculine superiority. She let him carry on because she was attracted to him. He remembered how he had once showed Josephine how to throw a knife. He aimed it for a circle drawn on the side of the barn. He missed the center but hit close enough to count. He walked over to retrieve the knife and just as he pulled it out…

THWACK! Another knife was thrown into the circle in front of him. He turned to see Josephine looking bright eyed and confident, suppressing a mischievous laugh. That's when he knew. This one was different. This was the one.

They raced horses through the woods, neck and neck, before Josephine pulled ahead. He grinned and admired her backside, telling himself that he let her win. But it didn't matter. Even if she was better, his ego was a price he was willing to pay to wake up next to her.

In an age of proper etiquette, the fast-advancing soldier ignored propriety and married a woman that people might whisper about as "a foreigner." John didn't care. This was a matter of love and he couldn't give a damn about the gossip. Besides, she was strong and beautiful and had skills to which only he was privy.

In bed, Josephine kissed him on the neck. He slid down and buried his face in her warmth. Josephine arched in ecstasy. He moved back up and entered her. His lips found hers and they rocked back and forth.

95

"Major," a voiced called. "Major Singleton?"

John pulled himself awake. He had fallen asleep against the tree.

"Yes," he said, rising to his feet. "What is it?"

"Some of the men would like to rest, sir," the soldier said. "We've been digging since we got here."

"Where is Sergeant Hill?" he asked.

"Don't know, sir."

John rubbed the sleep from his eyes, embarrassed that it overtook him in front of his men. He looked at the young soldier and beyond to the rest of the men. He left the ridge and strode back quickly to the worksite. Some were still digging, while others were asleep from exhaustion.

"If this war were up to me instead of the English, I'd give you biscuits and molasses and a bed of straw!" he yelled. The men rose from their slumber and returned to work with new intensity.

"You either dig now or the English will dig a hole for you," John reprimanded. He jumped into a hole, picked up a shovel, and dug alongside them.

For its part, the British encampment was also on high alert after hearing the distant explosion. General Ross and Admiral Cockburn had pulled up stakes and were moving through the camp on horseback.

"Corporal!" hollered General Ross.

A young man in a clean uniform came forward on horseback.

"Take a detachment back to Baltimore and investigate that explosion," he ordered.

"Yes, sir!" The soldier saluted and left.

"Aah, it's probably a local skirmish of some sort," said Cockburn. "Most likely something to our advantage."

96

"That was no *skirmish*, Admiral," replied Ross. "Could've been one of your ships."

"Bah!" replied Cockburn.

Ross turned to another of his men. "Get to the bridges quickly and send me a report. It will do us no good to continue if we don't have a way across."

"Our forces near Baltimore will still be able to do their business, General," Cockburn said in confidence. "Either way, we won't return home empty-handed. The British people will dance and call your name in the streets!"

"As long as they are not dancing on my grave, Admiral," said Ross.

Ross trotted away and Cockburn signaled to a soldier. A rough-looking rider came forward. An eye and an ear were missing, the result of a past encounter gone wrong.

"Take your men to the local villages," directed Cockburn. "Let them know we are here."

The man saluted. He turned to leave but Cockburn grabbed his arms.

"Set some fires," Cockburn told him. "That'll get their blood up. And bring me back some local preserves, or jelly. Something sweet."

The soldier nodded and left. Cockburn breathed deeply through his nostrils and coaxed his horse forward.

11 WASHINGTON

News of the English invaders and the distant explosion ricocheted through the hills and valleys and frayed the nerves of the commoners. The city was in a state of panic not experienced since the Revolution gripped the land a generation prior. Lanterns and torches lit the way as men, women, children, slaves, animals, rich and poor all converged on the roads. Wagons piled high with belongings streamed out of the city. The rich in wigs and parasols in their decorated horse-drawn carriages; the poor with their livestock tied behind them – all on the move.

From inside the capitol building, staff removed boxes of documents and loaded them into wagons. Gloved hands carried a parchment to a table as extra precaution was shown for the Declaration of Independence. The men carefully rolled it and placed it in a cylinder tube.

"Quickly!" a voice warned. The Declaration was loaded into the back of a guarded wagon with other cylinders full of important papers. A soldier saluted the driver and the wagon made for safety.

While the people of the city streamed out one side, Major Singleton and Sergeant Hill continued their preparations for battle on another. The few cannon they were able to secure were dispersed among the troops. Sergeant Hill bent down to inspect one closely.

"Not much range for this size," said Hill. "They won't shoot far, but it'll sure slow 'em down. Especially if we pack some shrapnel."

"See to it, Sergeant," replied John. "We need to do more than just delay them."

A boy carried a ladle and a bucket of water. John stopped him and took a drink. Suddenly, the boy dropped the bucket when he heard the sound of drums in the distance. John and Hill looked toward the sound across the valley.

They saw the torches first. Small slivers of light that pierced the early morning gray. American soldiers stopped what they were doing and looked toward the sound and the torches. Many looked frightened, for this was it. When the sun came up, they knew that it might be their last.

These Americans were not ready for war. John and Hill had done what they could and arrayed them in defensive positions, mustered with any weapon available, praying that the American regulars would arrive soon and save them. But the two men knew the stark reality ahead from their days as regular army and the unwinnable situation handed to soldiers throughout history by other men who would live to see more days. They were now past the point of alternatives.

Using his spyglass John could see at least a thousand Redcoats arrayed in front of him, followed by their weapons of war, cannon and cavalry. The drums announcing their entrance continued unabated. John assessed the long day ahead and its odds of survival for some and the last for many. He looked across the lines to see if he had any runners yet. He recalled a lesson on a no-win situation, when an American scurried from his hole with an expression full of fear.

Sergeant Hill saw him, too, and pulled out his pistol.

"Soldier!" he yelled. "Keep your place!"

The man didn't stop and Hill took aim.

"Stop!"

Hill fired just as John knocked the gun away. The man was hit in the shoulder and fell to the ground.

The soldiers looked in alarm at Hill and John.

"Hold your ground!" John called to the men who could hear him. "Fear will not rule the day here!"

"How are we supposed to fight them, Major?" a soldier dared to ask.

"Why, you liver-bellied--"

John grabbed Sergeant Hill by the shoulder to calm him, and turned to the soldiers around them.

"You think only weapons win wars?" John asked, and he shook his head no. "They will never win! Because your country called you and you came! Just as our fathers before us heard the call and won against all the odds! They feared as well. There is no shame in feeling fear! But you feel it, and you use it! Fight with your heart and with determination! Fight for your families and your country."

"This is the United States of America!" John continued. "Where one of us falls, another will stand! And, by God, we will make these invaders pay and send them to hell again!"

A cheer erupted. John looked at his soldiers and then across the valley to the enemy beyond – an enemy that was already going to work in other ways, in other places.

Unbeknownst to John and the defenders of Washington, a small group of men were spreading terror on the roads between Washington and Baltimore in the small village homes, country mansions, and farmsteads left undefended. Fire shot through the roof of a barn while the British soldiers emptied the contents. Screams and gunshots sounded in the distance as women and children fled for safety into the fields.

Josephine was familiar with the sounds coming up the road. She pulled her horse into the barn and closed the big double doors. She quickly led the horse to her stall and then climbed up to the haystacks stored in the loft above. Peering through a hole in the siding, she could see the riders and hear their voices as they sauntered down the road.

The riders were British soldiers armed with weapons and fire, and she instantly had dark searing images of a youth long gone in a far away country. She hated them. She was angry, not scared. Her temptation was to give in to the memories and to go out on the attack. But she remembered the Master's teachings and put distance between the hate and her actions. She would wait and let events unfold. It seemed as if the enemy had followed her to the new world. Those same Redcoats. They were here! And if they wanted her, she would make them pay.

The soldiers left the road and split up as they moved toward the house and the barn. One of the Redcoats opened the barn door and peered in with his torch. The livestock consisted of Josephine's horse and two milk cows, and they protested the sight of the stranger. The soldier decided to loot the barn first and he threw his torch to the ground. He grabbed a rope and tried to retrieve the horse. The horse reared away from him neighing for help from her master.

Josephine dropped down silently from the haystack while the soldier busied himself with roping the horse. She raised both pistols.

"Why would you take what is not yours?" she asked in French.

The soldier startled and turned toward her. He looked at the guns, then sized her up as a woman.

"I come here for peace, and still you must go places you don't belong," she continued in French.

"Come now," the soldier said. "Easy! I don't understand a word you're saying, but I don't need to. We are just passing through, lass. There is no need for this."

He slowly moved toward her. "Put the guns down," he beckoned. "There is no need for us to be enemies."

Josephine sighed, turned the pistols in her hands, and offered them to the soldier, grips facing out.

The soldier smiled again. "You see, that's much better," he said reassuringly. "We can be friends, no?"

"No," answered Josephine.

He came closer and, in an instant, Josephine twirled the guns again, barrels out. Without warning, she fired.

The soldier, shocked, looked down at his chest and the blood squirting out. He staggered back and collapsed.

"For your king, and your country," she said to him in English. He looked at her and died.

102

The horse whinnied for Josephine as smoke began to seep into the barn. She peered out the barn door and saw the criminals setting fire to her home. She mounted her horse and grabbed a pitchfork on the way out.

Josephine rode out of the barn, straight for the one nearest to her. When he turned toward her, she reared back and deftly aimed the pitchfork. *WHUMP!* The soldier fell backward impaled by the pitchfork. Josephine watched the fire race up the roof but didn't see...

WHACK! The gun barrel knocked her from the horse. She hit the ground and Cockburn's soldier was on top of her quickly. He pulled her up from behind, yanking her hair. Blood streaked down her forehead. He looked at her with his one good eye – the other was an empty socket – and sneered.

"You like to play it rough, eh bitch?" he growled, and he smashed her in the face.

Josephine was dazed, hurting, she spit blood from her mouth. He yanked the shirt from her back, and paused when he saw the scars.

"Well, I see you like a little pain--"

The fateful pause was just enough for Josephine. She turned and kicked him aside the head. He fell sideways and she rose to her feet. They faced each other, both equally enraged. He came at her and swung. She ducked and punched him with all her power in the groin.

"Aaah!" he screamed in pain.

When he lurched and fell, she smashed him in the face with a stomp. Blood ran from his good eye and he tried to get to his knees. She pulled his knife from his waist belt. She paused to catch her breath when she saw another soldier exit the burning house with his arms full of her possessions. He was just a boy, young and stupid, and stopped in his tracks when he saw Josephine. She was a figure of death. Her shirt was torn and blood stained and her breasts were exposed. He looked at her and she at him. Josephine took the knife and plunged it into the brute's neck. He fell for good.

The boy dropped the stolen goods and made for his horse. Josephine pulled the knife out of the man's neck. The boy jumped on his horse and kicked it into action. Josephine twirled the knife expertly in her hand and then launched it at the escaping rider. *WHUMP!* Directly in his back. The boy soldier fell forward and then from his saddle. The horse galloped off without him.

Josephine ran inside her burning house. She quickly retrieved one of John's shirts from the bedroom and put it on. In the kitchen, she pulled up the floorboards to reveal the box with "LL" inscribed on the lid.

She allowed herself to take a last look around the burning home; the painted picture of a man and woman on the wall, fresh flowers in a vase, and a book on a small table under the window. This was the only place she had called home since she was a young girl. She resolutely hefted the box up and left the house.

Josephine whistled for her mare. She strapped the box onto her horse, then hopped into the saddle. She wanted to turn around for a final look. To believe this wasn't happening. She hadn't asked for any of this. She had come to live in peace and have children and grow old. None of this was her fault. And now, her home burned and whether he wanted it or not, John was going to get her help.

Josephine rode off and didn't look back.

12 BRITISH ARE HERE

British soldiers moved into formation and loaded their weapons. Cavalry mounted and readied for charge. General Ross viewed the American opponent through his spyglass. The bridge and the road was guarded but undamaged. Their absence of munitions and reserves were in stark contrast to his own bounty of weapons he had brought with him. It was not often that a general could see such a prize ahead of him without shedding a high amount of his men's blood to get it.

"Take position!" Ross barked.

Soldiers double-stepped and moved into place.

"I want three formations," Ross demanded. He pointed, "Three! Here, here, and here. And I want the artillery ready immediately."

"Yes, sir!" replied the soldier.

Groups broke formation and moved to new designations. One took up the front while the others took up flank positions toward the bridge and the hill.

Cockburn rode up to Ross with his aides. The Admiral was now quite a sight to behold, sitting astride his white stallion, adorned in his gold-laced hat and rear-admiral epaulets.

"Admiral, are you not concerned that you will draw some fire?" asked Ross.

"Don't worry, General," answered Cockburn. "I always look my best whether I meet the enemy or my Maker. However, for your own safety, perhaps you should keep two lengths away."

Cockburn observed the American line with his own spyglass.

"See there," he said. "Look at this rubbish, General. They have not the slightest respect for our presence. I see no colors showing. I see..beards, General. Grizzly, dirty beards."

"I've never known a fighter with facial hair to be any less dangerous," answered Ross.

"Aah, you are fooling with me, General," replied Cockburn. "I know you know. They don't have any regulars! Let's hurry up and finish this."

"Steady, Admiral," said Ross. "Let's not throw opportunity away with too much hastiness. Where's my galloper?" He gestured to one of his aides. "What is the word from our scouts?" Ross asked him.

"Only limited movement, sir. And it appears that Washington is being evacuated."

"No, no," answered Ross. "Baltimore. Where are the regulars from Baltimore? The marines?"

"It is our understanding that the regulars are still *in* Baltimore," answered the aid. "Barney's marines are unaccounted for so it is entirely possible they are making way for our location."

"Hah!" Cockburn chortled. "There you have it. Now they are playing catch up."

General Ross was in utter disbelief about the lack of defense of the American capital. Not in all his years on the European fields of battle had a capital city been found to be so exposed. He allowed himself a little surge of excitement. Perhaps providence was on their side this day after all.

"So be it," said Ross. "Set the men in order. Ready for advance. On the double."

The aide saluted and backed away.

On the other side, Major Singleton and Sergeant Hill were setting their men to the ready when a shot rang out. John and Hill ducked and then looked toward the British line for the source. The Americans pointed their rifles, ready to respond.

106

"Hold your fire!" yelled John, and Sergeant Hill repeated it down the line before noticing the object of the enemy shooter's aim.

"There's what they're shooting at, Major!" Hill yelled.

He motioned to John to indicate the riders approaching. It was President Madison, Secretary Monroe, and Secretary Armstrong, alone but for a few aides. Madison reined his horse to a stop and put his hand out to an aide. The aide immediately gave him his spyglass.

"Really, sir, you must take cover," the aide admonished the President.

The President ignored the request and examined the British line. Another shot zinged by them. The President lowered his spyglass and looked down the American defensive line, the only thing standing between them and the British. The President looked back at Armstrong, who cowered behind his horse.

"Is this all the available men called out?" asked the President.

"Yes, Mr. President," answered Secretary Armstrong.

"Where is General Van Ness?" asked the President. "General Winder?"

No one answered.

"Do we not have any generals on the field of battle?" exclaimed the President.

The President looked at Monroe with exasperation, then dismounted from his horse.

"Given the situation," said Secretary Armstrong, "might I suggest that we change our strategy and plan to lure the British into the city. There are many places of advantageous position there. The House of Representatives is especially--"

Another shot clipped the dirt near the President.

"That's it," said Secretary Monroe. "I suggest we get our guns, gentlemen, and make ourselves at home."

"For an elected cabinet to take arms--"

"Get down off your horse, Armstrong," yelled Monroe, "before you become a casualty of war while sitting on your backside!"

John approached as their words grew heated. "Mr. President," John saluted.

"This is Major Singleton, whom you met earlier," Monroe said.

"Yes, I know that," snapped the President.

"Sir, forgive my boldness," John began. "This is no time for you to be up here."

"Where is General Winder?" the President demanded.

"I thought he was with you, sir," John answered, confused.

"To think what history will make of this," the President muttered to no one.

"Regardless, Mr. President, one thing is clear," said John. "We can only hold them here for a time until reinforcements arrive. But if you are killed or captured while spectating, we will lose more than a battle."

Madison hesitated to heed the advice, but then agreed with a nod. "Very well," said the President.

A look of relief spread across Secretary Armstrong's face.

"Barney's men will bring cannon with them, Major," Monroe told him. "When he comes, I recommend that you set them along the tree ridge. That should give additional cover to your force and get their attention."

"Of course, Mr. Secretary," John agreed.

"You are our protector between here and the capital, Major," said the President. "Until we find General Winder or the Commodore arrives, you are in charge. And God be with you."

The President extended his hand and the two men exchanged a handshake. The President then looked at the men, most of whom had never seen the President before.

"May God bless each and every one of you this day!" called out the President. "And the United States of America!"

He remounted his horse, turned around, and left with Secretary Armstrong and the aides following close behind. Secretary Monroe hesitated to leave as Sergeant Hill approached.

"Major, it is against every bone in my body to suggest this," said Secretary Monroe. "The British are in a striking formation and will attack soon. Should you need to retreat before reinforcements, take the Baltimore road and save some of your men. We will regroup with our forces there."

"Understood, Mr. Secretary," said John, "but there will be no retreat here."

The two men exchanged salutes.

"Angus, try not to be a hero," the Secretary said to Hill.

"Much obliged for your advice," Hill replied.

Sergeant Hill tipped his cap and Monroe rode off. Many of the American soldiers watched the men from the distance. Now they waited for John and Hill to order them to their deaths.

"Major?" said Hill.

John looked toward the British line, not answering.

"Major Singleton?"

"They walked quite a ways to get here, Sergeant," said John. "If their Captain has any merit, he'll know we're not ready."

"What do you think about Monroe's suggestion?" Hill asked him. "About a withdrawal?"

"We would lose just as many men and with greater futility," answered John. "We engage where we are. Our ground is higher and the British will have more open space to cover. With what little advantage we have, we can at least take some of them with us."

"Yes, sir," Hill replied and saluted.

On the British side, General Ross checked his pistol, then holstered it. A wagon filled with boxes of charges and shot rolled to a stop and soldiers began unloading. Ross dismounted and approached the largest contingent of troops. They stood to attention.

One soldier knocked a spoon against his rifle. Then another made a similar knock against his rifle. Soon, all the British soldiers were *rattling their rifles*, the drums joined in, and the sound of impending battle filled the valley.

John, Hill and the Americans looked across toward the ominous sound. There was no avoiding it. There was no ignoring it. Some of the young soldiers hunched down in their freshly dug holes and cried. The horses pawed at the ground for release. Old farmers spit their tobacco and watched. The rest loaded their weapons and gripped the barrels with sweaty hands.

On the British lines, General Ross raised his hand and the rattling died down.

"Attention!" a British soldier called out. The soldiers came briskly to attention as far as could be seen. This was the work of a professional army – years of drill and cadence and bloodshed.

"Gentlemen, we have come a long way for King and Country," said General Ross. "Years from now, no one will remember your months at sea, the poor food, and the endurance of miserable weather. History may even forget your names. But today, today is about something bigger than all of us. Today, this day belongs to the brave!"

General Ross remounted his horse and looked at Admiral Cockburn. He unsheathed his sword and ceremoniously thrust it into the air. "This land once belonged to your fathers. Are you ready to take it back?"

The soldiers *roared* their approval. Cockburn smiled at Ross. "Good show, General."

On the American side, John and Sergeant Hill loaded their own weapons and took up positions with their men.

"Keep your arms at the ready!" demanded John. "Do not waste your shot until you can see their eyes!"

"Steady, boys, steady!" Hill added.

John looked at the youth near him. The boy was barely bigger than his rifle.

"Stay low to the ground," he advised.

"Yes, sir," said the boy.

The British tore open their artillery boxes. A series of Congreve rockets were unpacked and shoved at an angle into the ground. General Ross watched from his horse and waited. Admiral Cockburn was almost delirious with anticipation.

A soldier looked at General Ross for an order, and the General nodded.

"Ignite your rockets!" yelled the soldier.

They lit the fuses. British soldiers covered their ears and ducked. The rockets blasted off with a high-pitched scream.

"What kind of devilry is this?" Hill asked incredulously.

"Rockets!" John yelled in response. "Take cover!"

The battle began with explosions and fire. Dirt and rock rained down on the men. The boy stayed down in the hole and hugged his rifle tight. John emerged from the dust to see several of his soldiers lying twisted on the ground amid the fire and smoke.

The British prepared to launch another set of rockets as some of the Americans abandoned the field.

"Hold your positions!" yelled John.

General Ross observed the chaos through his spyglass. "Concentrate on the center," he barked. "Once more!"

111

The next volley blasted into the sky with red trails screaming behind them. Explosions along the American line tossed the men about like dolls.

"Bring up the artillery!" yelled John.

The few pieces of artillery available were rolled into place, already packed and prepared.

"Send the bastards straight to hell!" Hill commanded.

"Fire!" John yelled.

BOOM!

Explosions ruptured the British line.

"Send some skirmishers forward!" Ross ordered.

A group broke from the British lines. They picked up speed and ran toward the Americans.

"Make ready, men!" said John. "For your home! Your country!"

American rifles were set.

The British skirmishers reached the bridge.

"Fire!" yelled John, and a volley of gunfire erupted.

Several British soldiers were stopped and killed at the bridge.

"Reload your weapons!" John ordered. "Artillery on the double!"

The command was repeated down the line. The cannon were packed.

General Ross again lifted his sword in the air. He looked at his foot soldiers for acknowledgement. Ross lowered his sword and the British moved forward and down the hillside – orderly and purposefully.

When Ross raised his sword to a ninety-degree angle, his cavalry appeared on the hill. Swords were unsheathed in unison; horses pawed at the dirt.

"Second artillery on that hill now!" Major Singleton shouted in warning.

The remaining American cannons were moved and aimed toward the hill. Rifles were set. With his small hand, the boy soldier pulled back the big trigger.

General Ross, assessing the situation, grew confident in the outcome.

"All forward!" he yelled. "More rockets, now!"

The British cavalry entered the field behind the foot soldiers, while a second group of Redcoats advanced toward the bridge.

"Fire!" John yelled.

BOOM!

The American artillery raked the British cavalry. Men and their horses spilled to the ground. Ross answered with another volley of Congreve rockets. They found their marks and exploded in the American lines.

"Fire!" John yelled again.

The American soldiers unleashed gunfire while more rockets rained down on them. Men screamed in agony as the American forces cracked.

The British skirmishers rushed across the bridge.

"Reload your weapons and continue firing!" John commanded desperately. "Fire at will!"

Rockets and gunfire exploded along the lines. John sensed a rocket before he saw it. He looked up, then instinctively hit the dirt.

After the explosion, there was pandemonium. Screams and death. John staggered to his feet through another haze of dust and smoke. The American line was teetering on collapse.

"Hold your positions!" he yelled, but he couldn't hear his own voice above the din.

British troops poured across the bridge and a group of Americans moved from their positions to stop them.

"Widen the circle," General Ross commanded. "Control the bridge!"

He turned to Cockburn. "I'll see you on the field, Admiral."

When the words were barely out of his mouth, a bullet cut through Ross's jacket, just missing his flesh. Ross stuck a finger through the hole and looked at Cockburn.

"You see," Cockburn said grimly, "today is our day, General."

Resolute, Ross galloped off, followed by a detachment of cavalry.

"That's the spirit, General," Cockburn said watching him go.

Cockburn trotted his horse forward. Suddenly, a bullet sliced through his stirrup and hit his aide. The aide fell off his horse, dead. Another aide hesitantly approached the Admiral.

"Admiral, I urge you to take cover!" he beseeched.

"Nonsense!" said Cockburn. "The war is in this direction, sir!"

The Admiral rode toward the action.

In the remaining American frontline, a group of soldiers formed near John under the constant shower of bullets.

"Sergeant Hill?" John shouted.

"Right here, sir!" answered Hill, as he quickly aimed and shot down an approaching British soldier.

"Barney's men are here, Major!" Hill yelled.

John looked back toward the tree line and saw that a division of American regulars was finally moving in. *Cheers* erupted along the ragged American lines. But was it too late?

Pipes and drums played above the noise as the British cavalry advanced.

114

John cocked his gun. "Follow me!" he directed.

A group of Americans lined up and moved with him, loading as they marched.

"Wait until my order!"

The British cavalry moved closer.

"Make ready!"

The Americans continued their advance.

"Aim!"

The Americans stopped, kneeled down, and cocked their weapons, one set above, one below. The British covered the field; the white of their eyes were upon them.

"Fire!!"

A barrage of gunfire rang out. The first line of British horsemen fell from their mounts. A second line quickly replaced them and continued forward. The Americans had no time to reload.

"Fix bayonets!" yelled John. They fixed their bayonets quickly with determination fueled by fear. "Hold your positions!"

The enemy horses ran through them and the marauders were met with bayonets and swords.

A Redcoat leaped onto John. They rolled to the ground, and John wrenched his pistol free. He blasted a hole in his assailant and rolled the dead man off.

"Major Singleton!"

John spun around. It was the boy, pointing to where the Americans were retreating – running for their lives.

Another British foot soldier ran at John and they embraced in a battle to the death. A sudden *explosion* knocked them both off their feet. When the smoke cleared, John was on his hands and knees, bloodied and bruised. His British adversary lay in two pieces nearby. John looked around and saw the grisly chaos of war playing out in all directions.

The boy tried to reload his rifle. He looked up just as a Redcoat was charging at him. John realized the boy was not going to make it. He looked on the ground for a weapon, anything, and saw a knife. In a split second he thought of Josephine and her abilities and how she taught him to throw a knife better than he ever had.

John grabbed the knife from the ground, rose to his feet, and flung it with as much force as he could. The knife sunk into the back of the Redcoat and dropped him. John and the boy looked at each other when another *explosion* interrupted the field.

When the smoke cleared, the boy lay on the ground with his left leg gone. He looked shocked at his condition and the bleeding stump. He looked pleadingly toward John, who moved to help the boy. Before he could make it, a shot hit John in the back and exited his belly. A look of anguish crossed his face as he grabbed at the wound and fell back down to his knees. The world was spinning, and the noise seemed to die away. The Redcoats were still coming and the boy was in trouble. John ignored the pain, grabbed a rifle from the ground, and tried to push himself back up.

Sergeant Hill saw that John was down and hurried toward him. He grabbed a rifle from a fallen soldier and fired it at an enemy. He couldn't reach John so the old soldier took his knife from his vest and screamed in anger to get the attention of the Redcoats around him.

John weakly raised himself to his knees as British soldiers ran past him. *Gotta get to the boy.* He was almost to his feet when he looked at his wound and the blood pouring forth. He felt a strange calmness in the storm now and he forgot the boy. There was no sound but violence all around. Something was different, and his dying thoughts turned to Josephine. *Oh, Josephine. I'm sorry, love. How much I miss you.* He sensed someone standing near him. *Josephine? Who is it? What are they saying?*

And then he fell.

13 DARKNESS

Josephine pushed the mare to its limits. They came to a branch of the river and she saw the bridge jammed with evacuees. She directed the horse into the river, dismounted, and hung on the side. The beast thrashed against the water as it carried them across. When they reached the bank, Josephine remounted and took off through the woods past a stream of refugees.

On the other side of the city, Commodore Barney's marines joined the battle. With his navy scuttled, he was pent up with more anger than usual and determined to extract the proper cost from the Redcoats. His sharpshooters went right to work with a blanket of fire raining down on an unfortunate group of British. The old sailor ordered the rest of his men to the tree-lined hill with their heavy cannon.

"That's it! That's it!" he cried. "Rough seas ahead, men! But we're gonna push these bastards back in the ocean!"

Barney chewed his tobacco until the juice streamed down his chin. He assessed the field from astride his horse and didn't like what he saw. The Redcoats had the initiative and sent the Americans running in all directions, yet Barney looked intent on putting up a new and stiff opposition. When a group of Americans broke for safety, Barney rode into the midst of them.

"You there," he yelled. "Get to attention! The marines are here! This battle ain't over yet!"

A loud *cheer* went up and the men turned back to rejoin the fight. They shot at any Redcoat in their sight. Barney rode to the cannon under a hail of gunfire. The men loaded them and set the trajectory.

"Let 'er rip!" Barney hollered.

BOOM!

A group of Redcoats were shattered and the cannon blasts gained Ross's attention. He saw the new player on the field and accepted the challenge. He pointed his men in Barney's direction.

"Fifty-first forward!" he commanded. "Fifty-first forward! Bring up the King's Own! Quickly!"

He grabbed the nearest aide by the collar and pointed. "I want that bridge controlled, not destroyed! And see that tree line? Those are the only regulars on the field!"

Immediately, British soldiers moved in formation to different locations.

Barney's men adjusted the aim of their cannon. The old sailor smiled at his sudden popularity with the British.

"Man the decks! Man the decks! Rough seas ahead!" he yelled.

The British sent a force forward. Dragoons closed in. Barney saw them coming and spit out his anger. "Send those bastards to hell!"

Barney's eighteen pounders exploded with a loud *BOOM!* The blasts ripped through the advancing British.

"Fire!" yelled Barney again.

Gunfire riddled the invaders. Amid disarray, the advance halted. Seeing this, Ross charged into his own men and set them into a firing line on the spot of Major Singleton's former line.

This time, the British fired. Barney's marines were hit, but more marines came forward to take their place and continued to load the cannon. Barney looked behind his position and saw other American units retreating. He spit out his tobacco in protest.

"Well, goddammit!!" he cursed and unsheathed his sword. "It's up to the marines to hold 'em here!!"

Ross dismounted and walked the field, seemingly oblivious to the battle raging around him. He strode among the casualties with his aides following close behind.

"Get the reserves up and make a wide turn," he ordered an aide. "Flank them on the east. They've got nowhere to go."

A drummer sounded the order.

Nearby, Barney pointed his sword to begin his own charge.

"Move in! Move in!" he barked. "Don't wait for them. Dig the rats out!"

A battle cry filled the air and the marines charged from behind the trees. Barney looked to his flank and saw the approaching danger: a regiment of British were coming in quickly.

"Watch your back!" he yelled. "Turn her into the wave!"

BOOM!

A group of Barney's marines turned to face the new threat and saw General Ross himself. They quickly set to a formation and reloaded, but it was too late. *Gunfire* erupted and raked through Barney's men. Smoke enveloped the field as Barney raced to aid his men. A lone bullet caught him in the hip.

"Jee-sus Jehoshaphat!!" he screamed, and tumbled from his horse. He tried to get up but couldn't, and his horse abandoned him. He looked from his position on the ground to the left. The British and his marines clawed away at each other. To the right, the British were advancing with few losses.

"Sound the retreat!" he yelled. "We can't stem the tide!"

A bugler played and two young marines rushed to help their fallen leader. He pushed them away. "Leave me be, you idiots!" he yelled. "Get the hell outta here!"

"No, sir!"

"That's an order! Get your arses out of here. Now!!"

The marines ran off and Barney laid back down, feeling the pain of his wound.

"Well, hell's bells," he said to himself. He checked his blood-soaked leg and felt around in his pocket for his pipe. The stem was broken from the bowl.

"Aw, damn them to hell," he muttered, and threw the pieces on the ground.

It was some time before gunfire was replaced by the groans and labored breaths of the dying and wounded. By dusk, those Americans who could had escaped into the city, leaving their fallen brethren behind. British soldiers stepped through the debris and corpses, looking for comrades and taking souvenirs from the dead. General Ross comforted one of his wounded men while Admiral Cockburn bent down to inspect the uniform of a dead marine.

"I knew it!" he said. "My God, I knew it was marines. Did you see the way they fought?"

Ross noticed a man in the same uniform crawling at a snail's pace. As he walked over to him, Barney heard the approaching footsteps and turned around to see who it was.

"What the hell do you want?" growled Barney at his enemy.

"Stay down, Commodore," Ross cajoled. "Don't you know when you've been beaten?"

Barney stayed down only because he had no choice. His hip was shattered and he couldn't get on his feet.

"You are Commodore Barney, aren't you?" Ross asked him.

"That's for me to know and you to find out," Barney answered defiantly.

General Ross smiled at him. "It is such a shame to meet in this way," said Ross. "I so admired the courage of your men. You shall, of course, receive full pardon."

Barney raised an eyebrow in surprise. Cockburn walked over to join them.

120

"I believe this is the Commodore," Ross said to him. "Commodore, this is Admiral Cockburn."

Ross left the two men and Cockburn looked down sympathetically at Barney.

"The legendary Barney," he said. "I would rather we had met in the open water, Commodore."

"Lucky for you we didn't," replied Barney.

"Maybe you will get your chance again, sir," Cockburn said. "No man of the sea should end his life upon the land."

Admiral Cockburn removed his hat and knelt down next to Barney. "A right honorable show, Commodore. One can always depend upon the marines for a good fight."

Cockburn examined Barney's hip wound with a quick look. "I'll see to it that you are cared for," he said. "Would you prefer to go on with us to Washington, or shall I send you to recover back in Bladensburg?"

"Aw, hell!" coughed Barney. "Send me back to Bladensburg."

"So it shall be," said Cockburn. "Bring up a stretcher!" he yelled over his shoulder. Cockburn smiled and tipped his hat to Barney, then walked away. Barney lifted his head and watch the Admiral go.

With the Americans routed, the only item purchased with the loss was time. The city was open and exposed and the next battle was a question of strategic importance. Does one give up the city or fight it out? Is it better to take a stand with what one has or stall and build a better defense someplace else?

The White House was fully alerted to the threat at their doorsteps. Servants removed silverware and paintings as soldiers stood guard. A framed oil painting of George Washington looked down over the proceedings. A soldier entered the room and handed a letter to Mrs. Madison. She opened it, read it, and covered her mouth.

"Oh, my," she said. "The President tells us to leave the White House without delay."

She looked around the room at the heavy blue draperies and the fine furniture. Her eyes rested on the George Washington painting. "They'll not have that!" she said. "Take it down at once!"

Two workers began to remove the painting from the wall.

"Get the President's papers," she ordered another.

"Yes, ma'am," answered the servant.

The First Lady walked into another room. The china, the fine curtains, the furniture. Where to begin. *Oh, what a disaster this is!* she thought.

She grew flustered and returned to watch the work proceed on the Washington portrait.

"Do be careful with it," she exclaimed.

"Leave it, Mrs. Madison," said a servant. "There's no time."

"I'll be damned if I leave it for them," she replied haughtily. "Everything else here is replaceable. I will not give them such treasures so easily."

The servant was surprised at her reaction and saw a tear run down her cheek.

"I'll burn it myself before I give them the satisfaction," she said with conviction.

The worker pulled and tugged at the back of the painting.

"The frame is bolted in, Madam," he told her. "Won't budge a bit."

She went to a drawer, removed a carving knife, and offered it to the worker. "Cut it out of the frame."

He hesitated.

"Do it!" she ordered.

122

He took the knife and cut along the frame, then stopped and looked back at her. She nodded and he continued cutting. Another servant entered the room.

"Madam, the table is still set for guests," he said. "Should I--"

He was interrupted by shouts of frustration and dissent outside.

"Where's little Jemmy?" cried a voice.

"Hang the bastard!" cried another.

As Dolley Madison fanned herself to abate her fear, a rock broke through a window and landed a few feet from where she stood.

"My God, the world's gone mad!" she exclaimed.

The soldiers hurried out of the room to disperse the angry crowd outside.

"I imagine I'll have to cancel the dinner engagement," she said to no one in particular. The servants exchanged surprised looks.

When the sun dropped below the horizon, the city was nearly empty of its people and many of its treasures. The first few survivors straggled in from the battle and expected to find some comfort and a new battle line. Instead they witnessed a hurried evacuation and had little choice but to join the exodus themselves.

The ground they left behind had been lost and remained littered with the dead and the dying. The remains of a house and crownless trees still smoldered while riderless horses ambled amid the scene, sniffing at the ground for something familiar. English soldiers roped them and pulled them into their ranks.

A group of surviving Americans too weak to walk sat together against a tree and out of the way, staring at the ground as British troops tossed the corpses of their fallen into a wagon. General Ross continued to check on the wounded of both sides. He noticed a pistol on the ground and picked it up to examine. A British soldier approached.

"Sir, all are accounted for. We are ready to continue the march."

Ross looked in the distance toward the capital and the dim speckles of light. How often does a man take stock of what lies before him? he wondered. Of the moments before his destiny changes?

"Find my horse," he said, handing the pistol to the soldier.

At the White House, a servant shut the front doors and stood at attention. A soldier assisted the First Lady into her carriage. She stopped on the carriage step and looked at the street, filled with people in a hurry.

"Madam?" asked the soldier.

"It is such a shame the President has to see things like this," she said sadly.

She climbed in and the soldier embarked behind her. Another soldier jumped up top and the carriage left. When Dolley looked out at the White House, she wondered if she would ever return. The carriage joined the crush of other residents leaving just as Josephine entered the city. She made her way through the exodus, and noticed the soldiers with their dejected faces toward the ground. She looked for John in the crowd. Not seeing him, she worked to get the attention of a soldier or two.

"I'm looking for Major Singleton!"

A soldier shook his head silently, either not knowing or too embarrassed to say anything. She stopped another soldier.

"I'm looking for Major Singleton!"

"Maybe here, maybe Baltimore," he answered dejectedly. "If he's alive."

She was considering his statement and weighing her options when a carriage drew near. She knew it was the presidential carriage and moved her horse aside. As it rolled past, the two women gazed at one another and their eyes locked for a moment. The First Lady, born to privilege and position; Josephine, a product of difficult times and war – two women whose paths crossed, connected by events, traveling in different directions.

Josephine hesitated and thought of heading toward Baltimore, but she knew John and knew he would not be there before his men were. She continued on to the front, dismissing a feeling of dread and fear she thought she had buried long ago. She stayed close to the street and observed the soldiers in

124

the crowd as they passed by. She looked at each face, searching for John's. With each unfamiliar face, the feelings swelled inside of her. She neither hoped nor prayed; she already had too many doomed expectations in her life. Yet, seeing the soldiers, she knew she had to be ready, to brace herself for what would be beyond her control. She recited her mantra and continued searching the faces. When she saw no more faces to examine, she turned from the road and headed in an alternate direction for the battlefield.

By nightfall, the streets in Washington had emptied of the last stragglers. Anyone with the ability to leave was gone; those with less to lose by staying barred their windows and doors and waited. A pack of dogs crossed the dark avenue as a group of riders galloped straight toward the White House.

One rider jumped down and ran up the steps. The others exchanged furtive glances from beneath their hooded ponchos. The rider pushed opened the door and went in, coming back out very quickly.

"It's empty, sir," he said.

Secretary Monroe lowered his hood. "Take the flag down," he responded.

The rider dashed to the pole, cut the rope, and caught the flag as it fluttered to the ground. President Madison looked out from beneath his poncho, grimacing at the situation. "Let's go," he said.

The President, the Secretary, and their escorts galloped off. The Capitol, the Treasury, and the White House were now abandoned to the next occupants. A cat meandered across the front steps of the White House and sat down to licks its paws.

Darkness enveloped the city and the surrounding woods, hills, and valleys, yet the smell of gunpowder and fire hung heavy in the air. Josephine saw the small fires from a distance in the woods and she followed them. When she arrived to the battlefield, she saw the torches moving and could make out the shapes of the people moving about and the bodies they were looking over. Some of the dead were stacked in wagons while others stretched across the field. People bent over them looking into the frozen expressions for the faces of their loved ones.

Josephine dismounted and walked the field with them. She looked at the dead and recognized how they had died – bullets, fragments, cuts, bomb compressions. Some of the fallen were old with their bodies twisted grotesquely. Others were young and appeared almost angelic in their deepest of sleep.

She stopped abruptly at one body. She instinctively knew but didn't want to believe. The torch light danced across his face and she dropped to her knees.

It can't be! Please!

John was dead. He looked peaceful like he was not there but rather in a pleasant dream, far away from the battlefield. And she wanted to be with him.

It can't be. This can't be. It isn't fair.

She immediately remembered being a girl and expressing a lack of fairness to the Master. The extra training, the drills, the cruelty measured out only to her.

Fairness is a human concept, the Master answered her. *Only the weak and the dead expect such things.*

She looked up and saw others gathered in grief around their loved ones. A strong breeze threatened their torches but they remained by their fallen loved one. She looked down at John and felt her last irrational hope of this being a nightmare blow away. He was gone and she had been too well trained to feel sorry for herself. She felt sorry for him. For what he had lost. For what these people had sacrificed. And she curled up next to John and placed an arm around him. She wished to die as well. She cried in anguished sobs.

14 ENEMY AT THE GATES

A slow, measured drumbeat woke the remaining inhabitants, announcing the arrival of the British in Washington. A line of riders with torches hurried ahead as the long shadow of the enemy fell across the city. A dragoon of soldiers followed, with General Ross and Admiral Cockburn leading them. The Union Jack, their standards, and colors were all on display as the foot soldiers marched into the city.

Some of the city's old-timers came out onto the street to watch. Others peaked through window curtains. Some wore expressions of complacency; others appeared bewildered, frightened, and beaten.

Cockburn smiled triumphantly. "What's that smell in the air, General Ross?" asked Cockburn.

Ross looked at him and didn't know what to answer.

"Smells like the spirit of 1776!" Cockburn suggested.

The Admiral laughed at his own joke. From the windows of one house, a man and his family watched. As the soldiers passed, the man ushered the family from the window.

Ross glanced upward to a balcony that jutted out from the second floor of a colonial-style house. An older woman with two younger women looked down from the balcony and the General quickly realized it was a house of prostitution.

Cockburn also saw them and caught the eye of the madam. She gave him a hard look and said something to the younger women, who then went inside. Cockburn grinned and removed his hat with a flourish. "Where are your men, woman?" he asked. "Where's our welcoming party?"

"You'll get no such welcome here, you old codger!" she hollered back.

"Come now, madam," Cockburn cajoled. "I know you're skills at bringing pleasure to a weary traveler. But really, did your patrons not leave anyone to protect you?"

"You think I need protecting from the likes of you?," she shot back. "I know the likes of you! The papers tell how you prey upon the innocent. There may be no innocence in this house, but you'll get no opportunity to taste these goods!"

When the woman withdrew a pistol from beneath her skirts, some of the soldiers laughed. Cockburn couldn't help but admire her boldness. Ross watched passively.

"You have nothing to fear from a British soldier, madam," Cockburn told her. "It seems you are too fond of reading those papers that make devils out of us."

"I know a scoundrel when I see one!" she sneered.

"You are misinformed, but I admire your courage! A shame that none of your brave men are here to share it!"

"If General Washington were here, he wouldn't be so inclined to your company!"

"Madam, if General Washington were here, we would have to skip this foreplay and hurry into action!"

More soldiers laughed but General Ross gave them a stern look and they held their tongues. Cockburn tipped his hat to the woman on the balcony. She spit on the ground and hurried inside.

Without warning, a *shot* rang out and General Ross's horse fell to the ground. Soldiers pointed their rifles in different directions as the General was momentarily trapped by the dead horse. He kicked his leg free, rose, and dusted himself off. Cockburn was incensed and pulled out his own weapon.

"Where was it?" Cockburn demanded.

"It came from there, sir," said a soldier, pointing to an old two-story wood-framed house along the street.

Another horse was brought to General Ross while several soldiers pulled the carcass away from the center of the street.

"General?" asked Cockburn.

"No damage done," answered Ross. "But it is folly to stay in the street and invite more."

Ross climbed into the new saddle and looked at his dead horse.

"What a waste," he said. "Goodbye, old friend."

"Take a detachment and root out the sniper!" Cockburn ordered a soldier. "And burn whatever building he fired from! I'll not have a vanquished enemy taking cowardly potshots."

Cockburn turned back toward the brothel. "Or was it a woman who took that shot, madam?" No answer was given, nor did he expect one.

"Let's move on, Admiral," Ross suggested. "Sentries, to your posts. The rest of you have your orders."

As the British swarmed through the city and occupied the capital, Josephine was asleep in the field, still lying next to John's body. She dreamed she was in the middle of an orchard. The trees were heavy with ripe fruit and she picked one to taste. It was sweet, like honeycomb, and its liquid essence dribbled down her chin. She passed it to John, who tasted it and smiled. They picked more fruit and put them in a basket. Before long, the basket became too heavy and a hole opened up at the bottom. When the fruit spilled out, Josephine hurried to grab them, but they rolled away and she couldn't catch them. She looked back to John for help, but he was gone.

She awoke calling his name. Her tears had dried and her horse nudged her further awake with her muzzle. Josephine looked lovingly at John's face and wiped away a smear of blood mixed with dirt. She smoothed his hair with gentle hands and straightened his jacket. Finally, she tenderly crossed his hands over his chest and held them in her own for one last lingering caress.

She was heartbroken and alone. The two killers of the soul, yet she had been in this place before and she would not succumb quietly. Her anguish boiled inside and she stood up and untied the wooden box from the horse. It dropped to the ground and she opened it. Everything was there and there was no hint of hesitation.

Ignoring the cold night air, she removed her clothes and tossed them aside. She stooped naked over the box, paying no attention to the curious mourners who watched. She took out her warrior's suit and slipped it on. It still fit her like it was just yesterday. The ceramic shields protectively wrapped her body as they had done many times before. Then came her belts and sheathed swords.

Josephine positioned the swords on her back, the daggers and guns in her belts. When she slid the veil across her face, the warrior was reborn.

Other mourners stared with their mouths agape at her transition. She looked down at her husband one last time. He was handsome even in death, but she knew the essence of the man she loved was gone forever. Death is a stark reminder of many things, and her eyes betrayed the pain of living with more shattered memories. She bent down and touched his face one last time and then turned away.

She remounted and rode off. She never looked back. She was now the predator seeking its prey.

Along Pennsylvania Avenue, a house burned while soldiers ran in and out of other buildings grabbing their spoils of war.

Another contingent of Redcoats stood guard against a group of residents, who gathered to watch the scene unfold. A soldier lit a fuse that ran inside a government building, then ran for cover. With a loud *BOOM*, the building collapsed into a heap of fire and smoke.

"Aah, what a glorious sight!' Cockburn said, relishing the destruction. He turned in his saddle to see Ross's reaction. "Don't look so glum, General. Remember our Canadian friends? If only they could be here to witness this."

"A people can be pushed too far, Admiral," Ross warned.

"Let the men have some fun, Ross. Besides, there's no one left to witness it.

If we don't get the flames high enough, how are they going to see them from Baltimore?"

The Admiral was pleased with his own suggestion while the General watched his soldiers. They entered the newspaper office under a painted sign, "The Intelligencer".

"Break all the C's!" Cockburn hollered at them. "That publisher took great license in disparaging me."

The soldiers brought out tables of type and upended them, spilling everything onto the ground.

"Well, General, while the men go about their work, why don't we pay little Jemmy's house a visit?"

Ross did not want to leave his men, and he did not completely approve of the Admiral's penchant for vandalism. "I'm going to look for supplies, Admiral" said Ross. "I'll catch up with you shortly thereafter."

"Alright, General," Cockburn replied. "Always the soldier. Very well, you know where to find me."

Admiral Cockburn tipped his hat to General Ross, and he and his contingency turned their horses toward the White House.

"Finish this up," General Ross ordered an aide.

"Yes, sir."

On the outskirts of the city, Josephine rode in the woods along a darkened road. She heard riders and stopped to observe from her concealed position. Four British soldiers trotted by at a slow pace. After they had passed, she quietly coaxed her horse to the road and followed them.

She was a stone's throw away when one of the soldiers sensed something and turned in his saddle. He saw her dark figure and could barely speak.

"What in hell--" He stopped his horse and turned. The other soldiers follow suit.

Josephine stopped as well and waited for them. The soldiers looked at one another in confusion. She was as dark as the night and an unsettling image. Two reached for their guns.

"Make yourself known!" one of the soldiers called out.

They caught a flicker of movement and heard a brief sound that cut through the air.

THWACK! THWACK!

The two outside riders were stabbed in the chest with the daggers. They each grabbed futilely at the assaulting weapon, tipped over, and fell from their saddles.

The two other soldiers pulled their pistols and fired. From their view, the figure on horseback did not move. Josephine knew their weapons and knew the likelihood of hitting her in the dark at this distance was small. She also didn't care if they did.

She slapped the mare with her reins and charged at them. The soldiers fumbled to holster their guns and pull their swords.

She pulled her own sword and passed between them with a slicing motion. She reined the horse around, and stopped. The remaining soldier watched in horror as his mate's head hit the ground with a sickening thud; the rest of the body soon followed.

Josephine observed her handiwork from behind her veil. The stunned soldier looked at her and his will to fight evaporated. He frantically kicked his horse and rode away in terror. *You would let many of our men fall while two of theirs yet live?* Josephine slapped her mare with the reins and took after him. She quickly gained on him and he screamed when he saw the demon bearing down. She raised her sword high; his mouth was still open in a scream when she removed his head from his body.

While Josephine emptied the road of her enemy, Admiral Cockburn reached the White House with his men. They set up a torch in a lamp post near the front steps and admired the beauty of the building; the tall stately columns, expansive windows, and neoclassical design. It was truly the palace of liberty.

A lone black servant came down the steps to greet them.

"Aah, there you are, Mr. President. I almost thought we had missed you," Cockburn joked.

His soldiers laughed

"Sir, the house is empty," the servant told him.

"Is it open?"

"It is locked."

"Well, do you have the key?"

"I do."

The men waited. The servant decided not to tempt fate further and turned to open the door. Cockburn appraised the mansion again, internally debating his future actions.

"It will almost be a shame," he whispered to himself, shaking his head. "Almost."

Cockburn trotted his horse to the foot of the steps and dismounted. He climbed the stairs two at a time followed by his men. The servant opened the door. When they entered, Cockburn removed his gloves and hat and tossed them to one of his aides. They lit the lamps on the wall and their eyes took in the room. The Washington painting was gone, with further signs of a hasty retreat.

Cockburn looked around and smiled to himself. "Little Jimmy Madison!" he hollered. "Where are you?"

No answer came and the soldiers grinned at each other.

"Gentlemen," Cockburn said to them, "You may want to take a trinket or two home with you. This is one you'll be telling your grandchildren about." The soldiers grabbed lamps and left on their treasure hunt. Cockburn turned to the servant.

"Do you have any of that American whiskey?"

An excited voice called for the Admiral from another room. Cockburn and his entourage entered and found the dining-room table still fully set for a banquet. Roasted meat sat on a spit near the fire. Beverage and liquor bottles chilled in watery ice buckets.

Cockburn looked at his men, and a wide smile broke across his face. "God bless the Yanks!" cried Cockburn gleefully.

In short order, they consumed the meal and the spirits and had a roaring good time at the Madison dining table. One soldier wore the president's wig, obviously ill-fitted and the source of many laughs. Another soldier rested a boot on the table. The servant stayed at attention against the wall as if it were just another White House dinner party.

Cockburn rose from his chair. "Gentlemen, please join me in a toast," he said.

All rose and held their goblets high.

"To the health of the President," he exclaimed.

"To health!" they all chimed in.

"And may little Jemmy Madison find a warm bed with an ample bosom to sleep in tonight," finished Cockburn.

"Here! Here!" the men laughed and toasted.

As he was draining his glass, Cockburn looked up to see General Ross enter the room.

"Ah, General, join us!"

Ross looked around at the disheveled table and the fighting men contentedly patting their full bellies.

"Admiral, our job here is done," Ross said humorlessly. "We should wrap up and return to your ships."

"What's the rush, General? The army has vacated the city. Give your men an opportunity to enjoy the spoils." Cockburn was not ready to end the party.

"The Americans are regrouping. I have word that the government is massing troops in Baltimore."

Cockburn refilled his own glass and sidled over to Ross. "My good man," Cockburn chortled. "You are a helluva general but boring as a mate."

The soldiers laughed until General Ross glared at them. They fell silent and looked down at their goblets.

"I'll be at my field quarters, Admiral," Ross snapped. "I plan to leave while fortune is still on our side."

As Cockburn watched him leave, he raised his glass. "A toast," he said sincerely, "to the General who sacked Washington!"

"Here! Here!" they all responded.

A sudden *gunshot* in the distance caused a moment of pause. But then the wig slipped off its tipsy thief, resulting in another eruption of drunken laughter.

Outside the White House, General Ross mounted his horse and left with an aide. As they rode down Pennsylvania Avenue, they saw fires burning in several government buildings.

"No more fires," he said to an aide. "We're not savages."

No sooner were the words out of his mouth when they saw a group of British soldiers push a family roughly into the street and then throw a lit torch into the house. The children cried and hid their faces in their parents' cloaks.

"Yaaahhh!" General Ross hollered and kicked his horse. He grabbed one of the soldiers. The others immediately stopped their mischief. When another soldier ran out of the house with an armful of loot, Ross pointed his gun at him. The soldier dropped his treasures and promptly saluted.

"What's going on here?" demanded the General.

No one answered.

"Take that man into custody and give him seven lashes," he ordered.

His aide rode up and grabbed the looting soldier by the collar. Ross released the man he was holding and looked disdainfully at the rest of them.

"What is the purpose of this despicable behavior?" he demanded.

Still, no one answered.

"There will be no more looting of common homes!" the General shouted. "Private property is off limits! Any trespasser will answer to me!"

He holstered his pistol and looked at the burning house. It was too far gone and he could do nothing for the terrified family watching the senseless destruction of their home. Sucking in his embarrassment at the unprofessional conduct of his soldiers, he galloped off.

15 RED SKIES AT NIGHT

But for the soldier standing guard nearby, Dolley Madison was alone in the empty room of an old countryside mansion. Her tears flowing freely, she looked through a broken window pane and watched the red and orange glow of fires in the distance. The capital city was burning. She pulled her cloak snugly around her face and angrily dabbed at the tears with her laced handkerchief.

Some distance away, Madison and Monroe sat on horseback at the top of a hill. They watched the same glow dance in the darkness beyond. *Is this the end of the American experience? What will history record of these events? Will the British seize us and put us on trial, or will our fellow Americans have at us first?* The men were thinking the same thoughts but they did not share them. The Revolution had taught them that their work is never finished. As painful as the coming hours and days would be, they could not give up or give in.

Josephine followed the trail of the American wounded. The soldiers drug themselves toward Baltimore if they could stay on their feet. Some died on the side of the road. The rest broke no words and occasionally one would turn and look back toward Washington. But they were too weak and dejected to care. The dirt road meandered its way to the bottom of a hill where field tents had been erected for a hospital.

Those that couldn't continue turned off the road and stopped at the field hospital interlaced with campfires and soldiers waiting to be treated. When the dark rider approached, their faces turned from the fires and watched her. She dismounted and walked near the campfires, looking into tents for a familiar face. When her presence was realized, a hush fell upon the patients. She entered a tent and walked by the beds filled with the wounded. Doctors stopped in the middle of a surgery and a nurse dropped a small tub of water. Josephine appeared a mysterious threat until she removed her veil.

"I'm looking for Sergeant Hill," she said.

No one answered.

"I know," a quiet voice whispered.

She turned and saw the boy from John's last battle. There was a stump of bandages where his leg used to be. She came to his side and bent down while activity in the room resumed.

"You're looking for Sergeant Hill?" asked the boy.

"Yes. Is he alive?"

"He was when we got here," the boy answered. He pointed weakly out the flap to a nearby tent. Josephine kissed the boy on his forehead and strode out. She entered the next tent, which was filled with post-op soldiers. All eyes that were able were upon her as she walked into the middle of the floor and stopped. She bent down to Sergeant Hill, asleep on his cot with bandages on his wounds.

"Angus," she called gently.

Sergeant Hill woke up. He blinked his eyes and looked at Josephine.

"Josephine," he said, dazed. "Where's the Major?"

A tear fell from her eye as she sat beside him.

"Aw, damn," he said. "I knew it. I tried to get to him."

She nodded and wiped away the next tear that tried to break free.

"What a waste," Hill said with his voice breaking. "And old bones like me keep on livin'." Then he took closer notice of Josephine's dramatic change in appearance and her weaponry.

"Well, I'll be," he said. "We always knew. He knew. Something was different about you." He cleared his throat. "You weren't the teacup and biscuits kind."

"Where is the army re-grouping?" she asked him.

138

He looked her over again for even the old soldier had never seen a woman dressed for battle.

"The regulars are in Baltimore," he said. "We tried like hell to get them. Wouldn't budge. Now the Major--."

He held her hand tight. "It's not supposed to happen like this," he said.

"It never is," she replied.

"There was just too many of them, and too few of us," he said ruefully.

"Now there is one more," she said.

She released his hand and rose. "I have some unfinished business in the capital." She kissed him on both cheeks and turned to leave.

"Josephine," Hill called after her.

She glanced back at him.

"Victory belongs to love and perseverance," Hill told her in broken French.

She nodded in understanding. Many eyes watched her go. Hill lay his head back down and stared at the ceiling.

The mare carried her down the road, past many of the walking wounded, and through a dark evergreen forest. Veiled once again, Josephine leaned forward and let her horse do the work. The mare galloped over the earth and her nostrils pumped for air. They bobbed among trees and down dark paths, accelerating as one.

While the Americans regrouped in Baltimore, Cockburn and his men ended their festivities and prepared to leave the White House. In the middle of the room, they stacked furniture almost to the ceiling.

"I rather like it here," said Cockburn. "It has a sense of propriety about it. Such a pity. What do you think, gentlemen? Should we burn this symbol of Yankee rebellion?"

The soldiers looked around the room. Many were doubtful so Cockburn resolved to do it himself. He grabbed a torch lamp from the wall and tossed it on the pile.

"Finish it!" he barked at a soldier.

Cockburn left the room. Soldiers threw their lamps as the one lone servant watched from the corner. The blaze grew strong and lit up the room, and soon the flames were licking at Dolley Madison's blue draperies.

Cockburn mounted his horse and turned to see that the destruction had commenced. Smoke began to rise above and mingled with the plumes around the city. A window blew out and the flames escaped from their new exit.

Cockburn rode off with a feeling of satisfaction, his solders followed after him. When they were some distance away, residents, vagrants, and those left behind came out from the shadows. They watched helplessly from the street as the emblem of American greatness burned.

When the sun rose after the night's events, fires still burned and the remains of many of Washington's government buildings smoldered. The air was full of damp smoke that seared the eyes and choked throats. Drunken British soldiers were asleep in great piles along the streets, having no concern about the chance for foul play upon them. Some soldiers were up and cooking fires with pieces of furniture, brewing pilfered coffee and tea, and rolling tobacco. In the countryside surrounding the city, the fall of the capital could not stop the necessity for survival. Families returned to work in their fields as if nothing out of the ordinary had occurred.

The Presidential entourage spent a restless night at the old country mansion, waiting for news on the British and on their own army. There was a knock at the door and a young messenger in uniform entered.

"General Smith will be ready, sir," the messenger reported to the President.

Madison adjusted his shirt and secured his wig. He turned to Monroe, Winder, and Armstrong, who were now waiting for a response from the President. Madison nodded to the young man, who saluted and left the room.

140

"That settles it," said Madison. "If we can't cut them off, we'll make our stand in Baltimore. General Smith will take over there."

"But, sir--"

"General Winder, you've done your duty here," he said. "I'll take responsibility for the capital. Smith knows the lay of the land in Baltimore. You'll report to him."

"Yes, sir," the General answered dejectedly, then left the room.

"Mr. President! I cannot--"

"Secretary Armstrong!" the President snapped. Armstrong quieted immediately at the President's tone.

"Your resignation is accepted."

Armstrong's mouth dropped open but he managed to stifle a response. The President and Monroe walked to the front door. Monroe turned back to glance at Armstrong, then they left him in the room alone.

On the steps of the Capitol Building, British soldiers converged to trade. They compared and bartered their looted items between swigs from stolen bottles of liquor. Inside the building, soldiers broke glass cases and pocketed more trinkets of interest. Others admired the columns, the fine mahogany furniture, the statues, and especially a soaring bald eagle from the second-floor rotunda. Plush green drapes lined the long windows and shielded the interior from the morning light.

Cockburn and his aides entered the building. He found a group of soldiers conferring together and joined them. They saluted at the sight of the Admiral.

"I trust you had a restful night," Cockburn said.

"Yes, sir, no troubles to report," answered one soldier.

"Well then, what seems to be the delay?" Cockburn asked.

The soldiers looked at each other. One bravely spoke up. "Sir, respectfully, this may be taking it a bit far."

"And what on Earth do you mean?" Cockburn demanded.

The soldier was hesitant but continued. "All of the government ministries have been burned," he explained. "As ordered. But this? This is akin to parliament, sir. Imagine the extreme reaction if our enemies had encamped on and then destroyed Westminster or Buckingham?"

"Have you forgotten York?" Cockburn challenged. "Or Detroit? We are not the instigators of this war. There is a history here, sir, of backstabbing and insolence. You leave the politics to me and carry out your duties!"

Cockburn looked hard at the man. "Let them reap the fruits of their own afflictions."

The soldier still hesitated.

"Get on with it or I'll find someone else who understands the hierarchy of command!"

"Yes, sir."

The insolent soldier saluted and the others began breaking down furniture, tearing paintings off the walls, and building a stack for a fire.

Cockburn, satisfied with the outcome, ventured to another room. Glass cases displayed artifacts from the founding of the United States. He abruptly stopped in front of one when he noticed a British flag captured during the Revolutionary War.

"I shall liberate this and take it back to its rightful owner," Cockburn said smugly. He broke the glass with his elbow and removed the tattered relic.

As he left the building, Cockburn shoved the flag between his shirt and vest. Soldiers saluted as his horse was brought to him. He jumped on and turned around for another look at the grand building. Soldiers lined the exterior and the American flag was lowered from atop the dome and replaced with a British one. Cockburn nodded his approval and trotted off.

Inside, the destruction continued. Soldiers used ropes to pull down the heavier statues, watching them crash to the floor and scatter in pieces across the rotunda. Others set fire to the curtains and the flames quickly raced from floor to ceiling.

The noble eagle, its wings spread against a backdrop of fire, looked down on the destruction. While the soldiers were distracted in their activities, Josephine emerged from behind the eagle, veiled and ready for battle.

She leaped for a chandelier and swung down to the middle of the rotunda.

The surprised soldiers stopped what they were doing, dumbstruck by her mysterious presence.

With a quick flick of her wrists...*thwack*....her daggers slammed into the chests of two unsuspecting soldiers. They staggered and fell.

A soldier pulled out his pistol, but Josephine was faster and fired hers – again and again in rapid succession. Four soldiers dropped. Others ran at her. She grabbed onto a flag pole, swung around, and kicked a man squarely in his face. A shot rang out; she pulled the flagpole down, spun around, and the bullet splintered the pole in half. The same bullet ricocheted into the head of another soldier.

She hurled the splintered pole like a javelin, impaling another advancing soldier. Just one left now.

He swung wildly at her and missed. She backed him off with well-placed kicks to the face and belly. He jumped up and hit her veil, knocking it out of place.

She stopped momentarily to adjust her veil as the bewildered soldier watched in amazement. She resumed her attack, kicking and thrusting until he fell.

He grabbed a sword from the floor. She unsheathed one of her own. They dueled ferociously and she cut and sliced him until he was bleeding in several places. He was beaten but he wouldn't give in. She unsheathed a second sword and crossed them on each side of the man's head.

"Get on with it, bitch!" he growled. "Whatever the hell you are."

She stopped and lowered the swords. She backed up, inviting him toward her with a hand gesture.

"Aaaah!" he yelled, lunging at her with his sword. She deftly turned aside at the precise moment and skewered him. He fell face forward and she removed her blade.

In a matter of minutes, Josephine stood alone amid England's finest, lying dead at her feet.

The fire in the rotunda gained strength and threatened to envelop her. The eagle, the statues, the flag – all the cherished relics of a broken nation turned to kindling.

Above the Capitol Building, the smoke billowed in great columns and dark clouds rolled in and mixed with the morning fog, overpowering the attempts of the rising sun. The British army began its march out of the city. General Ross stood on foot beside the troops holding a handkerchief over his nose and mouth. When the troops passed, they saluted and he saluted back. Admiral Cockburn rode up and joined in watching the proceedings.

"What weather," said Cockburn. "Why in God's name they chose such a sullen place for a capitol I do not know."

Ross uncovered his nose and smelled the air just as a distant thunder crackled across the sky. "I sense a change in the weather as well, Admiral," said Ross. "Let's not let our good fortune here get bogged down by a swollen river."

"Yes," Cockburn agreed. "A good thing we started last night. I'm satisfied that the fires have done their work. It should keep them occupied for some time."

A soldier brought General Ross a horse, but he declined with a wave of his hand. "Tether him to the wagon," said Ross. "I want to walk out of the city."

"Yes, sir."

"Care to join me, Admiral?"

Ross did not wait for an answer and set off at a brisk pace. Cockburn looked miffed.

144

"Shall I get your walking boots, Admiral?" asked an aide.

"Some coffee will do," barked Cockburn. Cockburn jumped down from his horse and moved quickly to catch up with Ross.

As Ross walked by his men, they cheered. Before long, the cheer grew in volume and carried along the entire ranks of soldiers. Ross maintained formality, offering a salute to the cheering men. Even Cockburn admired the show of pride in a job well done, smiling and saluting as well.

The exodus from Washington was quick – regiment after regiment, soldier after soldier. From windows and doorways, the faces of beleaguered Americans peered out. Boys and girls raced through the smoke to catch one more glimpse of the Redcoats. Haphazard lines of soldiers were molded into shape by the drums that accompanied the exit of the King's army.

From her perch above the smoldering building, Josephine observed the retreating army and planned her next strike.

Meanwhile, a steady rain poured down on Baltimore Harbor as the city prepared to defend itself. Wagons of supplies moved through the streets while slaves and their masters worked side-by-side to erect defensive walls. In the harbor, the masts of Commodore Barney's sunken fleet floated just above the surface. Small boats unloaded supplies at the docks and raced away to safety. In their crisp, clean uniforms, Baltimore regulars stood guard from the harbor all the way to Fort McHenry. Further out to sea, the British were in charge; the fleet was waiting to be reunited and then take down Baltimore.

A steady drum beat filled the air and the residents of Baltimore cleared a path down main street. Survivors from the siege of Washington were coming into the city. Militia, volunteers, and a few regulars – all dejected, tired, and hungry – as far as the eye could see.

The residents gawked at the men and the men stared back. A unit of Baltimore regulars took up position in the road.

"Make wayyyy!!" a voice commanded.

The Baltimore regulars stood aside, clearing the road in the process, and saluted. A lone clap came from the crowd, and then another. Soon, the whole town cheered and applauded the fighting men from Washington.

When the clouds opened and the rain reached Washington, Josephine's horse whinnied nervously at the thunder breaking across the sky. She quieted the horse with a whisper and they took cover in a hammock of trees. They watched the departing British. The long line of soldiers pushing ahead in the rain to return to their ships and to the next prize. *Not now*, Josephine thought.

As the rain intensified, the British were soon soaked to the bone. The wheels of the carts of treasures, the bodies of their dead, and big, heavy cannons became mired in the mud. Some were abandoned, while others were pushed free with the combined strength of men and horses. While a few men were struggling with a cart, lightning struck. With a deafening crack, a tree split, toppled, and crashed its crown to the ground, pinning two soldiers in the process. Other soldiers moved in quickly to help.

General Ross watched from his horse as one of the trapped soldiers was extracted alive. The other remained pinned by the tree and unable to be budged. A soldier kicked at the feet of the unfortunate soldier, but there was no movement.

When lightning ripped across the sky again, Ross thought he glimpsed an apparition in the woods. The woman and the boy again. Ross turned back to Cockburn, wondering if he had seen it too. Cockburn, however, was searching for his flask.

"I can't see a blasted thing!" Cockburn complained.

Ross hesitated and then changed his mind about mentioning his observation, but a soldier was pointing toward the same place.

"Leave him," Cockburn shouted at the soldiers trying to free the body of the unfortunate soldier. "I am already soaked! A cup of hot tea onboard my flagship is the only thing keeping me occupied. We can reach the harbor by nightfall if we stop wasting time!"

General Ross leaned down from his horse so only his men could hear him. "Leave a few men to pull him out," he said. "But don't delay. We have no time to waste. And do a quick search of the nearby woods. I thought I saw something."

The soldiers saluted and left. The march continued with Ross and Cockburn leading the way. From the hidden hammock, Josephine watched. Lightning revealed the depth of hatred in her eyes and rain dripped from her veil. She did not move; she waited as like a lioness stalking her next meal.

The tail end of the British army rounded a bend and disappeared. The fog grew thick from the rain-drenched riverbanks. The detachment gave up the body of the helpless victim and raced to catch up. Two foot soldiers lagged behind in the process. With the troops out of sight, they wasted no time in setting their rifles down and trying to light rolled up tobacco. Josephine quietly dismounted and moved closer. They gave up on the damp tobacco and unbuttoned their trousers to relieve themselves.

From behind a tree, Josephine balanced a dagger in her hand and reared back. The dagger flew through the air – *thwack!* The soldier yelled as he looked down at the knife in his belly. He looked at his partner in anguish, then fell over and died.

The other soldier retrieved his rifle with his parts still hanging out. He scanned the woods. Josephine darted from one tree to another. He saw the shadowy figure and *fired*.

Nothing. Panting and scared, he quickly reloaded. He saw the figure again. She entered the road and unsheathed her swords. He was terrified at the sight of her and rushed to get his gun loaded. *Hurry dammit!*

He cocked and raised the rifle.

Where did she go?

"I'm here," Josephine whispered from beside him.

He reeled around, yelled, and fired wildly. She ducked and then slashed him with two quick motions. Blood ran from his fresh wounds and he dropped his gun. His eyes bulged at the sight of his veiled killer and then he fell to the ground. She stood over him and wiped her blade off on his jacket. She sheathed her swords, retrieved her dagger, and *whistled* for her horse.

While Josephine picked off the stragglers of the English army, the city's inhabitants began to trickle back in. President Madison, the First Lady, Secretary Monroe, and a small escort returned on the same roads from which they'd left, but without the carriage and concealed by hoods from the rain. Their horses trudged down the muddy road, past the pale and wet faces of others who had fled on foot and those who had opted on staying.

At the entrance to the White House, they stopped and the President dismounted first. He removed his hood and cringed at the sight. He gave his hand to Dolley, who took it and dismounted. She removed her hood, covered her mouth in shock, and whimpered.

The White House was a burned-out shell. Smoke rose from the ashes, and the front steps faced charred columns and an empty doorway. All they could do was stare in shocked silence.

How did this happen? The insult of it all. Madison mulled several responses but he could not undo the damage in front of him.

Residents crept closer when they saw the presidential party.

"What do you think now, Mr. President?" asked a sarcastic voice. "Absolutely fine job you've done here!"

Dolley shot an angry look toward the offenders but Madison ignored the taunt, never taking his eyes from the White House.

"Where's Jemmy Madison going to live now?" croaked another.

"Don't worry about him, mate. Worry about where we're going to bed tonight."

"Long live, King Jemmy!"

"The bastard!"

One of the military escorts had had enough and wheeled around toward the crowd with his sword drawn. Monroe pulled out his own pistol.

"Get out of here, you dogs!" screamed Secretary Monroe.

"No!" shouted the President.

Monroe and the soldiers halted their action.

"Let them be," said Madison. "When we can't stomach angry words, our actions will only be worse."

The crowd backed away, still looking at the President with obvious scorn and contempt.

The President walked up the steps to the White House with Dolley holding onto his arm. When they stepped into the shell, Dolley wept. Madison comforted his wife with a tender pat, and then left her to herself. He stepped over debris, charred furniture, broken glass. He looked through the empty window frames, edged with ragged glass shards. In the distance, he saw the ruins of the Capitol and other government buildings still smoking.

As he hung his head from shame and resignation, he noticed a brilliant white quill in the debris. It was his own pen, undamaged! He picked it up and studied it closely. Thunder swept across the sky and a look of determination replaced the sadness in his face.

The same thunder shook the British troops as they continued their march. Two more soldiers lagged behind the rear line, trudging to keep up with their comrades. Under cover of the remains of the storm, Josephine saw her opportunity. She coaxed her horse to a canter, quickly closing the distance between her and the enemy.

The two soldiers neither saw nor heard their assailant. She raised her swords and slashed them as she passed, continuing to look forward without looking back. The two fell backward and sank in the mud. The rest of the British army marched on, oblivious to their stalker.

Near Fort McHenry in Baltimore, General Smith stroked his beard with one hand and wrote a note with the other on the side of a map. Behind him, a window provided a view of the harbor and the British ships in the distance. He put his pen down and was stuffing a plug of tobacco from his pocket into his mouth when a soldier knocked and entered.

"The army from Washington has arrived, sir," the soldier reported.

"Is General Winder with them?" Smith asked.

"No, sir."

"Typical! I'm sure that bastard gave the President hell over this. And then he doesn't even show up. Barney, Van Ness, Singleton. Where the hell is everybody? Just find a ranking officer and send him in."

"That's the problem, sir. There seems to be no ranking officer present, sir."

General Smith glared at the soldier and spat tobacco juice on the wooden floor.

As night fell on Fort McHenry, men worked together under the light of lamp torches. Bags of sand and wooden walls of dirt concealed a maze of paths and hiding places for the defenders of Baltimore to move along the harbor.

Smith walked among them, followed by his aides.

"Keep the men out of sight," General Smith ordered. "I've got a plan and I don't want them knowing our forces. They're going to attack no matter what, but the less they know, the more foolhardy they'll be. We're going to have to take a hell of a beating from the sea. We'll just get through it and wait 'em out."

He approached a cannon detail and they saluted. "You hold your fire when the time comes and wait for a signal," General Smith told them. "You do not fire until ordered. Keep your head down and let the bastards throw us everything they want to, then we'll give them something back."

"Sir?" asked a soldier. "I don't understand."

"We ain't gonna beat 'em out there!" he snapped. "They'll have to come in here and pry us out. And when they do, that's where we'll gain the upper hand."

"Yes, sir." The soldier saluted, and Smith continued his review.

"Don't they teach strategy anymore?" he complained to one of his aides. "And I had to learn it in French! Any further word from the President?"

"No, sir," answered an aide.

"Just as well. They can't do anything for me here except get in the way."

150

General Smith turned and poked a finger in the aide's chest. "If you do hear, don't tell me. By that time, I'll probably be committed and I don't want another opinion confusing things. That's an order."

"Yes, sir."

"Go get me a report from Stricker and meet me in the fort."

The aide hurried away and Smith continued on his own through the defensive maze.

16 UNWELCOMED GUESTS

General Ross placed his cup of coffee back on its saucer. He and Admiral Cockburn sat at the rough-hewn table, eating sausages and hotcakes. An unamused farmer and his wife stood to the side, watching with barely disguised contempt.

"My, that is great pork, sir," said Cockburn. "Do you cure it yourself?"

The farmer nodded but said nothing.

"Mmmmm," Cockburn said with his mouth full. "Wonderful."

Ross finished his coffee, wiped his mouth on the napkin, and rose from the table. He took a few coins from his vest pocket and laid them on the table. "I know this has been an inconvenience," he said to the farmer. "I'll have my aide pay you for the cost of hosting my men before we leave."

Neither the farmer nor his wife responded. Ross tipped his hat. "Madam," he said to the wife, and left.

Cockburn gulped down the rest of his coffee. "I wish he would learn to enjoy such moments," Cockburn said to the couple. He pushed his chair back, rose and nodded to them, and followed Ross out the door.

The British army had spread out over the farmer's fields, with the troops in various states of battle readiness. Guns were cleaned. Uniforms were prepped. A nip of whiskey was poured in a tin cup for the lucky few. Tents were taken down and fires were stomped out. A small bit of respite was welcomed after a night of continual marching.

General Ross stood on the farmhouse porch and looked back down the road in the direction from where they had come. In the distant sky, vultures circled and he had to shake away more of the omens and superstitions he was prone to remember from childhood.

From a treetop, an American scout looked through his spyglass across the fields of British army. From his perspective, he assessed the strength and size of the army and made note of Cockburn and Ross standing on the porch. He pocketed his spyglass and climbed down the tree.

The sky was still cloudy over Fort McHenry and continued to mask the morning sun. A sharp wind forced General Smith to hold his hat against his head as he walked across the fort grounds toward the southwest bastion. Several aides followed, trying to keep their own hats from blowing away. An officer on the wall turned toward the General and saluted.

"General Smith, sir."

"What do we have?"

The officer handed him a spyglass and Smith put it to use. Cockburn's fleet was still there, at least most of them.

"No changes here, sir, but our spies report that the bulk of their army is encamped on Miller's Farm."

Through the spyglass, General Smith could see the Albion, Tonnan, Euryalus, and Seahorse anchored in the far reaches of the harbor – all the main British warships assembled with only one purpose.

"From Miller's Farm, Ross will most likely split off and move his men on North Point today while he is at full strength," Smith said. "They've still got the taste of victory in their mouths. We will let them keep chewing that fat, keep thinking they can pluck what they want."

He handed the glass back to the officer. "I expect the bombardment to begin this evening. At least, that is what I would do."

"We have three batteries ready," replied the officer. "But won't do much good until we get them closer."

"That is exactly the plan," agreed General Smith. "We will have to take the beating. Aim short and keep doing it. Make 'em over confident. General

154

Stricker will need to stop Ross at North Point. That's our immediate concern."

"One more thing, sir," said the officer. "My men have been talking with those who came in from Washington. The locals say there were about twenty British left dead on the road."

Smith looked askance at the soldier. Rarely did the British leave their fallen comrades.

"What is it? Injury? Disease?"

"No, sir."

"Well, goddammit, don't keep me guessing! Perhaps some of Winder's men picked them off."

"They say it was a woman. She's dressed like a demon. Or a raven or something."

General Smith took off his hat and slowly examined it, then carefully and deliberately placed it back on his head.

"Then thank God this *demon* is on our side."

As word of a mysterious killer became scuttlebutt among the soldiers, General Smith ordered Stricker's militia to engage the British in the woods near North Point. Stricker positioned his troops at the edge of the woods and along a picket fence to harass and slow the British. But General Ross had no intention of stopping. With General Brooke in the rear and Admiral Cockburn's ships at the ready, the plan was to combine both sea and land forces and take Fort McHenry. Then they would wait for Baltimore to capitulate to terms.

Another drum roll announced the British army's readiness for action and the soldiers arrayed themselves in an attack formation.

Ross could see an occasional American soldier or two in the woods, but no substantial forces were visible. Cockburn joined him.

"My God, these Americans are a frustration to me," Cockburn grumbled. "Look at this presentation."

Unseen by the two British officers, Josephine and her mare moved in under the cover of trees and overgrowth. She stood on her horse, caught a branch, and climbed into a tree.

"Bring up the cannon," commanded Ross.

Soldiers moved to their task and cannon were rolled up into position, then aimed, primed, and loaded. The Americans for their part, saw the cannon, changed positions, and crouched low.

"Fire when ready!" yelled Ross.

"Fire when ready!" repeated a soldier. The cannon fuses were lit.

An American soldier noticed Josephine in the trees and nudged his partner, pointing her out. They both stared in awe, forgetting the danger in front of them. Josephine motioned them to look toward the British.

BOOM! The forest exploded and the two American soldiers disappeared in the blast. A line of American rifles returned the fire. Through the smoky haze, the British line moved forward, took aim, and fired again.

Several more Americans fell and a *cheer* erupted from the British line, followed by another drumbeat. Josephine climbed down and ran for a more advantageous position.

"Advance the front!" shouted Ross.

The British advanced and crossed the picket fence; the Americans retreated deeper into the woods.

"Ah, a good show, Ross!" exclaimed Cockburn. "Everything looks well in hand with these farmers. I'll go back and pull up Brooke's men. He has been itching for battle."

"I'll do it, Admiral," said Ross. "I don't care if it rains militia. I want this mission completed. We'll either be in Baltimore or in hell tonight."

Cockburn smiled at him. "I like your spirit! Very well, General. I defer to you."

156

They saluted and General Ross trotted away. When he passed several of his men in the second column, they cheered their leader. An aide moved alongside Ross's horse to accompany him.

"Stay here," Ross said to him. "I won't be long."

Two British soldiers advanced through the woods in search of Americans. Josephine stepped out from behind a tree with a pistol in each hand. She shot both of them, picked up one of their rifles, and moved quickly to a large oak. A massive branch bent to the ground from its own weight. Josephine climbed on and walked up the branch toward the main trunk. She could not reach the next branch with one hand so she wedged the gun between her back and her swords. She climbed the tree with both hands free and took a position against the trunk.

From high atop the tree, Josephine watched her prey. Her initial goal was to get the bigger one, the older one they called Admiral. And he looked like the man years ago from the ship. The one that took the General. But she wasn't sure. And she couldn't get a good bead on him, but a clearing in the branches allowed her to find the other target. The one they called Ross. The shot would be farther but clear from the foliage.

Ross trotted away from the front line just as a church bell rang in the distance. He stopped and turned toward the sound and admired the scenery as he had admired the singing on the way to Washington.

Josephine raised the rifle. This wasn't the first English rifle she had shot but it was heavier than she remembered. She judged the distance, buttressed herself against the tree trunk, and took aim.

"I am the power," she whispered in French.

Ross took out his pocket watch and checked the time. The gunshot sounded in the distance just as he closed it. When the bullet hit him in the back, the force made him arch and he dropped the watch. When he straightened, blood trickled from his mouth and a look of resignation crossed his face. He couldn't hold on and fell from the saddle. His boot caught in the stirrup; he tried to stand up, but couldn't. His boot slipped out of the stirrup and the horse trotted away. Josephine observed from the tree.

Ross was dying and he knew it. With his bloodied hand, he unbuttoned his jacket and reached for the locket inside – a picture of a wife and child. He held it tightly. He coughed and his breathing grew short. The sky was blue and white and it reminded him of Ireland. Of pride. Of freedom.

The locket slipped free from his grip, and the General who sacked Washington died alone on the road.

Josephine searched for Cockburn but he had moved away in the woods and was nowhere to be seen. There was still time to get him, she told herself. Her mission partially completed, she threw the rifle to the ground and climbed down the tree for more kills.

17 FIELDS OF GOLD

A group of British soldiers surveyed a map with General Brooke, the next in command, after Ross. With Cockburn and Ross advancing through the woods, Brooke was prepared to march his men through the opening toward Fort McHenry.

"I want your men near the harbor before night fall," ordered Brooke. "We will have scant time to prepare for the siege. The bombardment is set to--"

Brooke stopped barking orders. A horse with an empty saddle approached down the road and trotted by. The rest of the men followed Brooke's gaze and he turned ashen.

"Go find General Ross," said Brooke.

For his part, Cockburn continued to push the line forward with no knowledge of the disaster that had struck. Bullets were zinging all around him yet it was the British pressing the advantage.

"Keep it up, men!" said Cockburn. "There is much to gain in Baltimore!"

A soldier led his horse through the lines of soldiers and approached Cockburn.

"Admiral! Admiral!" he shouted.

"Bloody hell! What is it, man? You can see I'm busy."

The man extended an envelope.

"What is this?"

The man looked away. Cockburn took it, tore it open, and pulled out the note. He read the short scribbled message: *GENERAL ROSS IS DEAD.*

The Admiral shuddered and put a fist to his mouth. From the envelope, Cockburn pulled out the blood stained locket.

Damn. It's true.

Cockburn replaced the locket in the envelope, and slipped it into his vest pocket. "How dare they," Cockburn muttered. "How in hell did this happen?"

"Admiral?"

"How far back is Brooke?"

"About five fields, sir."

"Bring up Brooke. Tell him to take over and speed up the advance!" Cockburn grabbed the soldier by his lapels. "And not a word about this until today's work is done!"

"Yes, sir!"

The soldier trotted away and Cockburn removed his sword.

"Forward! Forward!"

Cockburn rushed ahead of his own line and rode straight into a group of Americans. He cut down one with a slash of his sword, then pulled his pistol and shot another.

His troops moved up to protect Cockburn and hand-to-hand combat ensued.

"Come on, you Yankee devils!!" yelled Cockburn.

British drums played a faster beat and a battle cry went up. The Redcoats advanced on the left.

BOOM! British cannon ripped through the forest and scattered more American forces.

160

"Roll them up!" commanded Cockburn. "Quick time! Finish these bastards!"

The British soldiers pursued the fleeing Americans. Cockburn rode after them, a man possessed. He hacked with his sword and counted another victim.

And then...the dark figure of Josephine the warrior appeared on the chaotic scene. She jumped down from a tree and slashed and cut a group of British soldiers to pieces. Cockburn turned his horse and faced her.

What evil is this he wondered. *Yes*, he remembered; taking Napoleon on board his ship, her call from the shore. Josephine had a similar memory; her General being swept to sea in chains, the redcoated bastard from the ship.

Josephine drew both swords and easily cut a soldier in her way. She raised her swords toward the sky, beckoning Cockburn with open arms.

Cockburn hesitated. He was not a man prone to fear but he was a big target with only one cutlass. He also saw an opportunity if he would only wait. To her left, Josephine heard a rifle cock. She pivoted and deflected the *shot* with her sword and cast a dagger at the shooter. The shooter fell. She reared back toward Cockburn just as his bullet *slammed* into her shoulder.

The blow knocked her off her feet. The pain vibrated through her body and she felt the place of impact. A lucky shot between her ceramic plates. Cockburn holstered his smoking pistol and extended his sword.

"Yaaahhh!!" he screamed as he came in for the kill. Josephine used one sword to force herself up and the other she readied for Cockburn. He reared back and prepared to slice her. She moved out of the way and blocked the sword with her own. He came back around. She was unsteady but unyielding. He came at her again; she blocked with one sword and sliced with the other. She caught him on the thigh and the sword trailed through his flesh.

"Aaah!" Cockburn yelled in pain. He did not turn his horse for another pass. Josephine's mare, hearing her whistle, bolted through the forest and knocked into the admiral's horse. The horse stumbled from the impact and pitched him off.

The mare ran to Josephine, who latched onto the beast and allowed it to drag her away through the woods. Cockburn stumbled to his feet and watched as the horse carried his assailant away. Blood oozed from the crease in his leg and added to his vengeful mood.

With Stricker's troops in an orderly retreat, the British soldiers organized to hold their position. The rest of the men moved back to fall in with Brooke's men and prepared to advance on Fort McHenry. When they left the forest and crossed over the same fence and the field, they realized the high price of the day. Word spread fast of their fallen leader and the men grew somber. General Ross's body lay in the road, covered by a handkerchief on his face. Two soldiers stood at attention nearby. Passing by the body, the men removed their caps if they had one. Some cried in disbelief.

Cockburn followed behind on his horse, bruised and dirty from the battle and his uniform stained red with his own blood. Brooke rode up alongside as an aide tried to assess the Admiral's wounds.

"Are you alright, sir?" asked the aide.

"Where is General Brooke?" Cockburn snapped.

"Here, sir," said Brooke.

"The Americans are stalling us from here to Baltimore," Cockburn stated. "You will need to press ahead now, right now, while they are falling back."

"Yes, sir."

"I'll return to my ship. We'll focus on Fort McHenry as planned. Nothing changes!"

"Yes, sir."

"You are in charge now, General Brooke."

"Yes, Admiral."

Cockburn looked back at the woods one more time. "Damned devilry," he muttered. He looked at Ross's body and turned to an aide.

"Make sure he is returned to the ship."

162

"Yes, sir."

"And get me my surgeon and a clean pair of trousers."

General Brooke and the aide saluted as Admiral Cockburn rode away.

Meanwhile, at Fort McHenry, General Smith was handed a report from a heavily breathing rider.

"Have a seat," he said to the messenger.

"I'm fine, sir," he panted.

The soldier caught his breath while the General read the report. When he finished, he scrunched it into a ball and threw it on the ground.

"Goddammit!" he exclaimed.

His aides looked up in alarm. Smith paced the floor, looking out the window each time he passed it.

"Stricker's men have retreated," he said. "The battle will be here tonight." He stopped and turned to the men. "And we are not retreating!"

There was a knock on the door and a wounded soldier came in.

"What is it?"

"General Smith?" he said in a hushed voice.

"Yes. Speak up!"

"There is an addendum to the report," he said. "I rode as fast as I could. The British General was shot. He is dead, sir."

General Smith was stunned by the news – a fortunate turn of events indeed.

"General Ross?" he asked an aide. "It must be Ross."

"It wasn't one of ours who killed him, sir," said the soldier. "At least, I don't think so."

163

"Make sense, man!" Smith barked.

"The men say, well..."

"Talk!"

"They think it's a woman. She wears a black mask. Looks like a raven or something. Scares the hell out of the men. She shoots and carries a sword. Kills lots of the enemy. Damn good."

General Smith glared at the messenger and his officers gathered around him. "This is the second time I've heard of some mystical demon on the battlefield," he said. "I don't know what to believe and I don't care. The only thing I give a damn about is the strength of the enemy and how close they are. Until this demon starts killing us, I don't want to hear another word about it. Bring me confirmation that General Ross is dead, and prepare to send the rest of the bastards with him!"

With Stricker's men giving up ground, Brooke ordered his troops to clear and hold until the siege of the Fort was ordered. They combed the woods until dark for any American stragglers and then returned to ready themselves for the march. With darkness surrounding her, Josephine dropped down and lay on the bank of a nearby stream. Her horse stood patiently nearby, drinking from the cool water and resting. She removed her veil and grabbed her wounded shoulder. She rolled her face into the stream and took water herself. She looked at her reflection.

She removed her vest and breastplate and gingerly felt the wound with her fingers. The bullet had entered from the front and exited out the other side. She knew what she had to do, but she was weak and the blood had run free for some time.

She cupped her hand into her reflection in the water and poured its contents on her shoulder. She knew it wasn't enough and that she would need to act before the wound festered and the battled moved on without her. Through the woods, she saw a lone flickering light.

Inside a nearby farmhouse, a family sat around the table as the kitchen fire burned low. The woman laid out a basket of biscuits, a bowl of beans, and a platter of meat. They bowed their head in a silent grace and were about to eat when a different prayer was answered.

164

Josephine came through the door without knocking, startling the family. The farmer rose quickly to his feet. They were fearful at the sight of her.

"I only need your fire," she said in English.

The farmer looked at his rifle leaning against the wall, but Josephine was standing between him and the weapon. She quickly surmised his intention and grabbed the gun. She tossed it to him with her good arm.

"I only need your fire," she repeated.

The farmer took the rifle and nodded toward the fire as the family backed out of her way. She grabbed a poker near the fire and stuck it into the flames. The small boy and girl looked on wide-eyed with curiosity and fear. Her wound was open for all to see. She took the poker out of the flames and spit on it. It sizzled and she knew it was ready.

She motioned for the man to take the poker. When the farmer hesitated, his wife took it instead. "Look away," the woman told her children.

Josephine nodded to the woman, and she plunged the poker into the wound. Josephine *screamed* from the searing pain and the frightened children backed into a corner of the room.

After a few more seconds, the woman peeled the poker off of Josephine's shoulder. As she tried to look at the cauterized wound, Josephine collapsed unconscious.

In her dream, Josephine walked through the empty streets of her village and wondered where everyone had gone. Then she saw her mother, father, and brothers and sisters. A Redcoat had lined them up against a wall with several others.

"Josephine!" her mother called. "Run!"

The British troops fired. The dream turned dark.

"*I will teach you to understand any enemy,*" she heard a voice say in the dream.

Josephine, just a child, stood on a stump, blindfolded. She held a sword out to each side, in perfect balance.

165

"You will know their actions before they do," said the voice. *"Your mind will be power. Your sword will be death. Your coming will be feared."*

In the dream, Josephine was now older and saw herself riding through an enemy line. She shot and cut through them until their bodies dropped. She walked through the field of death and suddenly saw a familiar face. John lay dead with the rest. Josephine bent down to look at him, shocked at the sight. She moaned in pain. Did she kill him?

"There's that dark whore," said another voice. *"That black demon."*

Josephine awoke from the dream with a start.

"Easy," said the woman. "Sssshhh."

Josephine looked at the woman and the two children who stared at her, then at the man of the house. The woman patted her forehead with a wet cloth, and motioned for her children to bring a bowl of soup.

"You are safe," the woman said. She repeated it in French.

Josephine was surprised when she heard her native tongue. She looked at her wound, now wrapped in a clean cloth bandage.

"How did you know?" she asked softly in French.

The woman pointed to a place on her own neck.

"You have the symbol from the old world," the woman answered in French. She took the soup from the girl and spooned it into Josephine's mouth. "I remember soldiers coming through my village. I was very young. I have never seen one of your kind, though I heard stories that there were women among your ranks. I can only imagine what you have experienced."

The woman spooned another mouthful of soup to Josephine's mouth. "My children are so curious. Of course they know nothing of the old world. My daughter wants to know how she can become such a person. A woman who carries a sword."

Josephine turned her head toward the girl. "Do you understand me?" she asked her in French. The girl nodded. "Come closer," Josephine requested.
166

The girl looked at her mother for permission, then came closer. Josephine put her finger on the girl's heart. "This is your real strength. With this, you have everything in the world. You need no sword. No other weapon."

The girl managed a slight smile. The mother looked on, approvingly, and shooed the girl away. The two women shared a look of sisterhood.

18 RED GLARE

Munitions were stacked against the walls of the fort as a group of soldiers moved quickly down a prepared corridor, up a rampart, and to the outer walls. As they passed, other soldiers stopped what they were doing and came to attention. The soldiers carried a huge American flag and were being careful not to drop it. They reached General Smith, and stood at attention in front of him.

"It's about goddamned time," he barked. "Well, what are you waiting for? Run it up!"

The soldiers hooked the flag to a rope. They braced against each other and pulled hard, for the large flag was heavy. They inched the flag up the pole with each pull. The wind caught it, unfurling the stars and stripes.

Soldiers in their defensive positions around the fort saw it. Those along the shore pointed to it – fighters along the harbor, residents in the city, slaves, shopkeepers, women, and children – all stopped and stared in awe. The great flag reached the top of the pole and whipped in the wind. Shouts came from the fort and were joined by others coming from the city.

Out in the harbor, Admiral Cockburn arrived on deck with a limp and new trousers. All stood at attention. He grimaced as he took a spyglass from an aide. He extended it and when he squinted into it, he could see the fort and the ramparts built to defend it. And then he saw that damn flag. A look of defiance shadowed his face.

"Bring up the bombers," he commanded. "I'll show them the price of insolence."

A *bell* sounded on the ship. The fleet each returned the signal with their own bells and turned broadside to the shore.

American soldiers ran to position. Cannon were loaded and wheeled into place. General Smith moved quickly among posts followed closely by his aides.

"Stay away from the wall!" yelled Smith. "And be patient! Wait until after the first volley or you'll be a sorry sonofabitch!"

General Smith took his spyglass from an aide and leaned against the wall. He could see the British warships aligned and prepared for battle. "The Albion is making ready," he said. "Hell is coming." And a battleship *FIRED*.

"Down!! Everybody down!!" he yelled.

BOOM! The bombardment began with a blast into the eastern wall. *BOOM! BOOM! BOOM!*

The unfortunate victims of war were buried in rubble or catapulted to the sky. Men ran as the bombs smashed into the fort walls and toppled earthworks. Projectiles of brick, mortar, and wooden shards cut the men to pieces.

"Get those cannon firing!" commanded Smith.

Three cannons were packed and loaded.

"Keep your aim short!"

"Sir?"

"Do it!"

The fuses were lit and the men braced themselves.

BOOM! BOOM! BOOM!

Fire lit up the night as bombs crossed in the sky. They whizzed by the flag waving over the battle.

The American cannon blasts exploded in the waters short of the ships.

BOOM! BOOM! BOOM! retorted the British ships.

Soldiers tucked in or ran for cover as the bombs crashed around the fort. A wall toppled down on soldiers below. Cockburn monitored the siege through his spyglass and saw the caved-in wall. "Move our ships in closer. Adjust your aim and focus on that breach!" Cockburn ordered.

Two rowboats full of British soldiers raced for shore under the bombardment. The Americans met them with a barrage of bullets. Brooke's men advanced toward the fort from the beach with ladders, ropes, and weaponry. One of Cockburn's aides saw that the surge of men were too near the focus of the shelling.

"Sir, we should adjust our target," the aide suggested.

"No, keep it going a while longer," Cockburn replied.

"What of our own men, sir?"

"They'll have to get out of the way!"

General Smith watched the scene from the fort. He looked down at a platoon of soldiers huddled and poised for battle. He gave a signal and with a *battle cry* from the soldiers, they moved from the grounds of the fort and raced toward the harbor.

Brooke's men took up position on the shore in anticipation of the approaching Americans.

"Make ready!" he ordered.

The Americans charged.

"Fire!" yelled Brooke.

The Americans in front fell and those behind took position, aimed, and fired!

The British troops in the front collapsed yet Brooke beckoned his men forward with their bayonets fixed. Hand-to-hand combat ensued as more British soldiers arrived by rowboat. They took shots from their boats and then jumped into the fray.

"Artillery on the double!" yelled Brooke.

Brooke's men pushed and pulled their artillery through the sand to an advantageous position.

"Into the earthworks!" ordered Brooke. "And don't stop until there is no more to kill!"

Smith ordered his own cannon to adjust and they set their sights on the rowboats. One soldier cranked the levelers and another lit the touch-hole.

BOOM! The rowboat and its passengers were blown to bits. A *cheer* erupted from the Americans.

BOOM! Smoke and debris filled the fort and the American cannons rolled backward without their handlers. The blasting continued and Brooke ordered the combined forces up and into the breached wall. They brought the ladders forward and the Americans fought to stop them.

General Smith, knocked down by an earlier blast, pulled himself up and looked over the wall. With the British congregating in the breach, General Smith turned to his remaining men.

"Fall back!"

"Sir?"

"Let them over! Keep drawing them in!"

The soldiers moved back and cleared the bastion for the British troops. The Americans below were overwhelmed by sheer numbers and the first of the enemy climbed the ladders.

"Prepare to defend yourselves, your homes, your country!" yelled Smith.

The British clambered up the ladders and poured through the crumbled wall. The forces fell on each other with a vicious ferocity and the bastion filled with gunfire.

Suddenly...Josephine galloped into the fort. Fully armed, veiled, and with swords drawn, she again appeared as the grim reaper to the British. She

172

leaned down from the horse and sliced through a row of Redcoats as if they were butter.

The Americans saw her attack and surged back toward the British. General Smith slashed at a British soldier and shot another. *Shots* come from all directions at Josephine. She arched and twisted and cut her way through the invaders. When she ran over a group of them, they screamed at being trampled and their bones broken. General Smith withdrew his sword from a victim and looked to the bay. Cockburn moved his ships closer to the shore, and Smith knew his opportunity had finally come.

"Now!! Now!!" yelled Smith as he waived toward a distant hill.

More American cannons were unveiled from a camouflage of trees and rolled into place. They were lit, and they *fired*.

"Take this, you bastards," whispered Smith.

On board Cockburn's ship, an aide laughed gleefully.

"Admiral, the fort is ours!" he crowed.

Through his spyglass, however, Cockburn saw a different story. He saw Josephine on the wall – the black raven in the moonlight.

"My God," he said.

American cannonballs filled the night with a brilliant red glare. They climbed higher and higher, and arced across the sky. Disbelief washed over Cockburn's face. He looked off the bow for the impact.

BOOM! The shot slammed into the Seahorse. British sailors jumped into the bay to escape the flames.

The tide turned in favor of the Americans.

BOOM! Cockburn was thrown to the deck. A ship's bell sounded as more explosions rock the ships. Cockburn saw fire break out among his flotilla.

"Move us back!" ordered Cockburn.

"Sir?"

"Turn us to port!" exclaimed Cockburn.

"What of Brooke's men, sir?"

"They look to be dead or dying!"

"Turn to port!" the aide called. The aide backed away, then turned from Cockburn. The Admiral watched opportunity slip from his fingers – his paradise lost.

At the fort, British soldiers heard the ship bells. Brooke looked first at his men on the wall and then back out to the bay. He saw the British flotilla had turned away from the battle.

"Ah, that bastard," Brooke said angrily. Realizing his predicament on the beach, he had only one real choice left.

"Either you take this fort with me," he told his men, "or we all die here today!"

Brooke led them up and over the breach in the fort and into the thick of the fighting. They shot and slashed with intensity and pressed the Americans back on their heels.

Josephine dismounted and presented herself on foot. She ran at them with swords drawn. The Redcoats attacked her but she sliced and somersaulted through them; a rip here; a thrust there. She blocked a bullet with one sword and cut through bone with the other.

Brooke and his men reached the bastion in time to see the dark demon slaughtering their countrymen. Bullets ricocheted off her swords and armor as she whirled and fought. She singlehandedly crippled the attack, allowing the American soldiers to roar back into action. But the British, pressed with their backs against the sea, would not yield.

Brooke grabbed a second sword and motioned his readiness to Josephine. She advanced and they locked swords. The fighting intensified along the wall and a British soldier slipped through and cut the rope holding the American flag. The flag dropped to the ground. With the American colors down, the British renewed their fight.

"Get that flag back up!" yelled Smith.

Josephine backed Brooke on his heels. He gritted his teeth and stabbed wildly. She cut one sword from his hand and forced him toward the breach. She was close to finishing the job, when another soldier lunged at her. She relieved him of his breath with a thrust through the chest. Brooke pulled his pistol. He saw a gap in Josephine's armor and jabbed the gun in. They struggled over it, and he *fired*.

"Aahh!" Josephine screamed in pain.

She fell back and Brooke pounced. His hands were quickly around her throat.

"You're dead!" Brooke cried triumphantly, and he squeezed tight.

Josephine remembered the Cossack. She remembered the Englishman when she was a girl. She dug and scraped for a weapon as she felt weak and breathless. She found her dagger and thrust it in. Brooke grimaced and released his hold. He fell off her and Josephine grabbed her side where the blood spilled. She rolled over on top of him.

"Not today," she said, and pushed the dagger in deeper.

Brooke sputtered and died and she pulled the dagger out. She saw the flag lying on the ground. Through the breach, she watched the Americans and British, fighting and killing each other. She staggered to her swords and sheathed them, bumping into others in the heat of battle.

She picked up the flag and wrapped it around her body, dragging herself to the breach.

"I am the power."

She jumped. The wind caught the flag and slowed her descent. Cockburn saw her. Smith saw her. The soldiers from the ground looked up as she smashed into them.

She unsheathed her swords, and willed herself to kill more. The Americans rallied around her and together they advanced on the British. Josephine slashed and blocked. Her mantra rang in her head and time suspended. She was between life and death and her body acted upon its own memory.

175

Josephine was shot, stabbed, beaten, but she did not fall. Each blow was met with one of her own and she forced herself further into the den of the enemy. Blood ran free and the Americans and British fought for eternity.

From Cockburn's position aboard his ship, he saw the red glare of war and the tide rolling against them. And then he saw the American flag aloft on the beach. And then there was her. Killing his men. That damned devil was still there.

19 BRAVE

In the fog of the early morning dawn, wreckage and corpses floated in the water and blocked up the sea foam on the beach. The burning hulk of a British warship protruded from the bay.

Farther out to sea, the remains of the British fleet collected their dead from the water and tallied their losses. Onboard Cockburn's flagship, Ross's body, wrapped tightly in white cloth, was brought up to deck and laid next to others until the deck was full.

Near the fort, American soldiers moved smoking bricks and cast charred lumber aside to pull their own fallen comrades out of the carnage. Along the beach, four soldiers carried Josephine with great care, using the large flag folded as a stretcher. Other soldiers craned their necks to get a closer look. Many removed their caps and saluted her broken body as she passed by. Others grabbed onto the flag and helped to carry her into the fort.

General Smith removed his hat when they stopped in front of him. A soldier moved to lift her veil, and she managed to raise a hand to stop him. General Smith stopped him as well.

"She earned the right," he said. "Hurry up!" he ordered the men. They carried her away with other soldiers standing aside.

"Who is she, sir?" a soldier asked.

"A brave American," he answered. "And that's all we need to know."

The day and the battle faded away into the annals of history. Sunny and warm springtime weather returned to Washington and the losses in Baltimore became a distant memory. Flowers were abloom and the streets once again teamed with the hustle and bustle of a flourishing city.

Workers climbed scaffolding to rebuild the White House. Children played along Pennsylvania Avenue. The elected leadership returned to the damaged capitol. Bricklayers and stonecutters were hard at work on the government buildings and the city's elite stepped around them on their way to once again engage in the push and pull of democracy.

A crowd gathered in front of the White House as President Madison held up a proclamation of peace signed by the British government. Secretary Monroe and General Smith stood behind him, along with Sergeant Hill and General Winder.

As in most wars, the names of those who gave the orders would be remembered. The names of those who perished, of the dark warrior who emerged, would be long forgotten.

The crowd cheered and tossed their hats in the air as the White House was restored to its former grandeur.

On the outskirts of the city, Josephine sat astride her mare. Dressed in traveling clothes, she looked down over the city that was once her home. She rubbed the mare's cheekbone and suppressed the thoughts of her past, and of those things that could have been. With her wooden box tied to the saddle, she pulled the horse gently to the road. To where, she didn't know. To what purpose, she had none.

A group of robins moved together across the road and took flight from her approach. Josephine took flight as well, and never looked back.

> *"I am the power.*
> *My life is my own, my methods answer to no one.*
>
> *I am the power.*
> *I bring light to the dark, order to chaos, and fear to the fearless.*
>
> *I am the power."*

Finis.

ABOUT THE AUTHOR

Daniel Parker is the author of Downfall, and Leadership for the Quiet Revolutionary. He graduated from Florida State University with a degree in Urban Planning, and spent time in Russia with the United States Peace Corps. He was a six-year Planning Commissioner for the Tallahassee-Leon County Florida Planning Commission, with nearly 18 years in the public sector. He has facilitated several classes on sustainable living and spoken at numerous venues on smarter growth policies. He lives with his wife and three children in Tallahassee, Florida.

Made in the USA
Middletown, DE
01 December 2017